Paw-ly

Love

Paw-ly Love

Stories of Polyamorous Furs

Edited by Thurston Howl

A THURSTON HOWL PUBLICATIONS BOOK

Contents

Catch a Wave

Cedric G! Bacon

Jake heard the shouts of warning before the feline did.

Each year the last weekend of September always seemed to bring out that final push from the tourists. He couldn't blame them: with its sweeping fall breaks presaging the coming winter, Calusa Bay's middle of the road humidity proved ideal weather for the baggys, as Jake and the other locals called the tourists due to the trousers they all wore down at the dunes.

The swells that afternoon had been tasty, with everyone lined up and taking their turn as courtesy dictated. It could be a hard lesson learned if one invaded the spot of another, especially when someone was exiting a boom tube nose first with their board. Jake instinctively touched the deep and dark groove which broke up the gold of facial fur, with another long stripe going down his muzzle. Hard lessons, alright—surfing can be quite fabulous but dangerous if you were not on point.

He looked up to the horizon and saw Gina, the red squirrel lifeguard. She was scanning the horizon through her dark sunglasses, reclining in her perch. They had dated off and on since high school, and were now currently off. Their arrangements weren't exclusive or even serious, as he was well aware of Gina's preference for women as much as men. Jake never cared about that, and it never stopped either from being friendly towards one another. While she probably couldn't see him, Jake threw a waving paw in her direction.

Waiting for his wave to come, the canine's eyes went up and down the row until his wandering gaze fell on the feline immediately adjacent to him. A Devon Rex, her chocolate brown fur was touched by a chessboard of white spots, her long tail thwipping against her longboard in anticipation as remnants of the sea rolled off her lithe body in droplets, fierce determination raging behind her eyes. Jake added that she was very pleasing on the eyes, with long and pretty legs which belied her slight height, as well as a nice shape to her chest and butt areas, thoughts which caused Jake to blush deeply in his ears.

The Rex's spine straightened and her ears folded forward, having felt the Lab's eyes on her. She turned her head and she met Jake's gaze, and as usual there was the polite nod and smile, a quick acknowledgment of recognition. The more Jake thought about it, he could not recall seeing the Rex interact with anyone else among the surf crowds, getting the impression that the Rex was standoffish and aloof, preferring it that way to hanging out on the dunes with the rest. From the minute her board touched water to the moment she dipped out on land, the Rex was a blur of motion and difficult to catch up to.

So on this day, Jake was not certain what exactly happened: perhaps the Rex had thought she had the all clear when she took off into the tube. Or maybe she paddled out just a minute too early into the rolling wave, paws touching the aurora forged by the swell and shifting on her board as if she were flying. Everyone stopped and watched, another common courtesy afforded to the community, but someone shouted that she was about to wipe out and eat tide due to the quickly growing speck that gained form and shape on its approach towards her.

A ferret still aloft on his longboard had gone far out and caught the biggest swell back towards shore. Either everyone forgot he was out there or what, Jake didn't know, but he joined the rest of the group in shouting towards the Rex to get out of the way, her paddling and wading and waiting for the swell placing her in the direct forecast of the longboard. She gave no mind, waving towards the rest and only tilted her head at the strange gestures they were making towards her to move.

And when it happened, it was a sickening crunch of body on body, bone on bone and wood on wood as two riders went into the waves, their empty boards rolling with the tides. The ferret bubbled up to the surface, gasping for air, pissed off and cursing aloud at all the damnable luck and pointed around to everyone if they saw what had occurred to absolve any blame from themselves.

But as Jake looked around he let out a whine of anxiety as he waited for the Rex to appear. Seconds crawled by with the aching haunt of worry, until a minute had fully passed into a minute and a half with the Rex yet to resurface.

Taking a long and deep breath and not taking a second thought, Jake dipped below the waves, the sun becoming little more than a shimmering curtain on its surface and the black swirl of the endlessness raked across his skull. As his ears popped and throbbed with his beating heart and his eyes stinging from the saltwater, he scanned the blurry floor and hoped...well, why hope? He didn't know her, she didn't know him.

But she was a fellow surfer and that unified them, regardless of familiarity. The Lab's heart gave a leap of joy when he spotted her, floating in the middle of that bleakness, forelimbs spread limply. Jake kicked and swam as fast as he could to her, and thanked the fates that the Rex was still breathing, albeit shallowly, and there was the thready thud of a heartbeat beneath her chest. Getting back to the surface world was the main priority, and Jake took it, emerging with the Rex and taking many baleful gusts of the world's cool clean air as Gina and a group of other lifeguards helped him ease the feline onto the rescue board and back on land.

"Back up!" Gina ordered. "Give her some air!"

The crowd folded back as Gina performed CPR. Wrapping her snout around the Rex's, she breathed in then pushed hard and fast at the Rex's chest, humming the Bee Gees disco tune "Stayin' Alive" while she did. Soon, water erupted from the Rex's maw like a volcano as she coughed back to life, and a collective sigh of relief seemed to pass through everyone around. For Jake, he could breathe easy himself. He stood off to the side holding his board as he watched the red squirrel lifeguard explain to the Rex just what had happened.

She nodded solemnly and cut quick glances at Jake's direction. Their eyes lingered far longer than the courteous node and quick smile that typically passed between them, and Jake started forward, thinking he could say something.

But then the Rex's attention returned to Gina, then was helped up to her feet by the red squirrel, soon spirited away and up over the dunes, and soon out of sight. Jake watched when it was just the red squirrel who returned, and his ears dipped in disappointment.

Gina caught his eye and walked towards him. "Good work you did there, pup. You always were a good boy."

Jake wagged his tail then cleared his throat as he returned to normal. "You didn't do bad yourself. Is she gonna be alright?"

Gina cast her glances over the dunes and then returned her gaze to the Labrador. "I think she'll be okay. You know her?"

"No, but I was hoping to talk to her, check if she was okay," Jake said.

Gina grinned.

"No, not like that! I really wanted to make sure she was fine. Is she coming back anytime soon?"

Gina shook her head. "After something like that, would you?"

Jake sighed and said, "Guess not. Hey, what're you doing tonight anyway? Still seeing that cat of yours?"

Gina grinned then touched the side of her nose. "Why? Jealous?"

"I just thought, you know," Jake began, "maybe we can go get something to eat and then maybe hang back at your place afterwards..."

"Can't," Gina informed him. "I've got a date with that cat tonight."

Jake cursed his luck as he watched Gina walk away, then grabbed his own bag and board to leave. His ears perked up at the sound of lapping wood off to the side, and he followed it, coming across the Rex's temporarily forgotten longboard. He lifted it out of the water and wiped it free of the mud and sand, then slung it across his shoulder as he made his way up the hill to the parking lot.

He didn't see the Rex again for a few days after that. Just in case, he cleaned her board and kept it in the back of his car, keeping his eyes keen to the shore hoping to glimpse her again. When he did, she was sitting near the lifeguard looking out at the distance, seemingly cool to everyone who looked on her. A still healing bandage was affixed above her right brow, but otherwise she did not appear to be in any great pain. Riding back with the tide, Jake hopped off his board and made his way to the Rex's direction. He was a few feet from her when her attention was alerted, ears rotating like a satellite dish to Jake's soft footing and strong canine scent.

"Hi there!" he said brightly, planting the tail of his board into the sand. "You probably don't remember me from the other day, but I just thought I'd come by and check on you. 'Til that accident, you had the best ride I've seen in years coming here!"

She eyed him coolly, and there was a faint whiff of suspicion from her charcoal gray, wrinkling nose.

"Thank you," the Rex said finally, then quickly placed a digit inside her left cochlear, closer to where Jake was standing and made a circular motion as her head tilted to the side. "Sorry, I didn't hear you coming. But yeah, I remember you pretty good. I didn't get a chance to thank you for saving my life. Stupid me, should've been paying better attention."

"It's okay, as long as you're okay," Jake quipped. "It happens a lot. Heck, look at my scar here, it's a honey of a reminder that the surf can catch you and chew you up and spit you out just like that."

The Rex chuckled lightly at this and agreed. "Well, when mine heals up we'll probably be twinsies with our matching battle scars."

"Right on," Jake said, excitement ringing behind his voice as his tail wagged behind him. "Anyway, I just thought I'd come by and get properly introduced to you, since I'd seen you around and know next to nothing about you and..."

The Rex blinked once, still radiating a sense of concentration as she tried to hang on to his words and watching his lips move. And then it dawned on Jake why she likely had not heard everyone shouting at her the other day to get out of the way, or the odd movement of her digit inside her ear. And when the thought came to him, he briefly felt embarrassed for not picking up on the signals earlier.

Jake took notice of the tension which crackled from her body language, as if she was not certain at the Labrador's intentions. There was a vague hint of aggression, believing Jake would fail whatever test was being applied at this bit of introduction. He inhaled then sat down as close to her as allowed without giving into skittishness, looking her square in the face and spoke up a bit more, extending her an open paw.

"I'm Jacob, but you can call me Jake. Just so that we don't have to keep on being strangers to one another."

The Rex shook and cracked a smile, whiskers shining brightly in the glint of the sun. "Minamezcameron. Neesetameat yootoo, Jake." She grunted in frustration then adjusted the other ear, letting a sigh pass her snout. "Sorry. It's still sometimes hard for me to hear everyone and everyone to understand me. I can't surf or swim with my hearing aids in, they won't work right if they get wet. Anyway, it's nice to meet you too, Jake."

"You're doing fine, I wouldn't have known that you were deaf," Jake said, then quickly apologized. "Sorry, I don't mean to assume."

The Rex chuckled. "You canines are usually on the nose with your assumptions. Sometimes other folk get it all wrong."

"Can you read lips?"

"Still practicing," Cameron admitted. "I'm not good at it yet, but I'm okay at sign language. As long as I got my inner ear aids I'm golden."

"Cool stuff. But I won't take up your time, Cameron. I just wanted you to know you forgot your board the other day..."

The Rex's eyes lit up. "I thought I wouldn't see that again!"

Jake's tail wagged as he said, "I caught it before the tide carried it back out. I've got it in my car if you want to come over and get it. Obviously I don't need another board."

"I don't know," Cameron smirked, "I've seen your technique. You'd probably be a lot less shaky if you had more room to maneuver."

Jake returned the grin and said, "So is that an invitation to keep it?"

"Shit no," Cameron answered, ginning. "Give me back my shit."

Jake laughed and helped her up, as an easy fall breeze kicked up and brought the scent of the sea and salt to them. Walking back to his car, she threw out crumbs of conversation, primarily questions for Jake to answer and all centered around Calusa Bay's surf community and how long they both had been on their respective boards.

"I used to skateboard," Jake admitted when they reached his Hatchback. Popping the trunk open, there was Cameron's longboard, waxed and cleaned daily by Jake and gleaming from the sun's reflective rays.

"Ain't that the truth," agreed Cameron as she leaned against her board. Her eyes shifted to Jake's legs and butt for the minutest of seconds before they re-established eye contact. "I never could get into boarding on land, but I did notice you move like a skateboarder, all fanciness and shit. But you're good. Not Peggy Tsubo good, but pretty good in your own way. You've been coming here almost as long as me."

"Peggy Tsubo's a surf goddess," Jake agreed. "Glad someone remembers her and the old Dogtown surf team."

"You sound shocked," Cameron pointed out.

Jake shrugged. "It's just hard to find anyone else interested in a bunch of surfers and skaters from thirty years ago." Then, he added, "I always wanted to talk to you before, but I didn't know how to approach you. You always seem to scoot away when you get on land."

Some of the coolness returned to Cameron's expression as her ears folded over her head. She looked down and raked her paws against the grain of her board. The Rex began to speak, but the words came out slightly jumbled and she hissed in frustration with herself as she once more set the tip of her right forepaw into her ear and made a couple screwdriver motions.

"Damned thing," she snarled. "Sometimes it makes it hard to understand even myself half the time. But now you know one reason why I book it when I'm done."

"How deaf are you?" Jake asked.

Cameron nodded. "The docs call it sensorineural hearing loss. Got a bad fever when I was a kit and the nerves of my inner ear never recovered, so I missed out on a lot of sounds."

"How does that even work for you? You know, getting by without sound?"

Cameron held up her paw and spread her digits wide. "I can feel things through my pads or even the vibrations if the frequencies are loud enough. It's like being hosed down in the vibration of sound without hearing it. Kind of like surfing through soundwaves when you really aren't."

Jake had not thought of that before, and enjoyed the metaphor. He remembered his own temporary deafness from concerts, the blasts surrounding him even if he could no longer properly hear the music coming from the speakers.

"Well," Jake said, "I can understand you just right."

This elicited a smile from the Rex. "You sure can, and I'm glad that you can. Makes me feel pretty good. You're one of a few, I can tell you that much."

Jake was about to respond when, gripping the handle of his trunk after throwing his own board in the back, he pulled the door too low and bashed himself between the ears, seeing stars on instant.

"How you ever saved my life, I'll never know," Cameron said between laughs. "Are you okay?"

"Yeah, peachy," Jake whimpered, shaking some sense back into his head. "Well, I did my civic duty for the day. Hopefully I'll be seeing you tomorrow."

"Quick, personal question," Cameron asked. "If that's 'kay?"

"Sure," Jake nodded, "but I reserve the right to decline to answer if I don't like it."

"That's fair. What are you doing tonight?"

Jake stared for a moment at the frankness of the question,

although it was more of a statement.

"I can answer that," he began. "I've got nothing much going on, except reheated leftovers, talking with some online pen-pals, and a few hours of bad horror movies ahead of me."

"Ooh, sounds like fun."

"You don't need to patronize me," Jake laughed.

"I'm not! I really think that sounds like fun. But, if you're into hanging out later, I can give you some tips to help your technique."

"What's wrong with it? I've been surfing for years with no problem!"

Cameron shrugged. "You could tighten up your form, I think. Like I said, you're not bad for a skateboarder." The Rex then took the Labrador's arm and felt his bicep, then trailed over to his pectoralis. "Yes, good shape too. That upper body strength does you wonders. Do you swim?"

"I try and hit the pool when I can," Jake answered.

"I bet your breathing is amazing, giving you excellent stamina like Peggy Tsubo says in her book. You could probably do better with someone helping you."

Jake was taken aback. Not only had she just issued a perfectly clear invitation—masked in tones that could be viewed as a challenge—and he took his time formatting a response in his brain before opening his maw.

The Labrador's bemused struggle was not lost on Cameron, as she grinned up at him. "I'm serious, Jake! You should come with me tonight. That is, if those bad horror movies are calling to you."

"It's a good thing they're all on VHS," Jake laughed. "You're on!"

"It's a date!" Cameron exclaimed. "Come and meet me out here after closing time."

"You do know we'll get into trouble, right?" North Beach was typically open from 7 a.m. until 7 p.m. A local deputy patrolled the area in case any of the pups and kits decided to have too many shenanigans late at night.

But Cameron waved these concerns away. "My friend Gina

is the head lifeguard. She's offered to pull late night duty as long as we're in her quadrant."

Cameron was true to her word. Gina waved down at the pair when they walked past her station that evening, after the beach had closed up and everyone else had gone home. She specifically smirked in Jake's direction, as he shook his head, knowing the implication of that smirk. He realized nothing was going to happen between himself and Cameron: if it did, it sure wouldn't be happening on the beach late at night.

That stuff only happens in the movies, he thought and chuckled to himself.

As he followed closely behind the Rex, he took notice of her outfit. Cameron was dressed in a tight-fitting neon green halter top, though to Jake's eyes it was more of a dark hue, along with a pair of red stretch pants which gave her backside a pleasant, rounded shape. Still, his lack of the typical color cone-cells did not stop his gaze from studying the Rex up and down with all the furtiveness his breed could muster. If she caught him, she did not say anything.

She was also true to exposing all of Jake's weaknesses without even setting foot in the water as the pair made their way to a balance board that the Rex had set up ahead of time on the basketball courts. She helped him onto the balance board, holding his ass and thighs tighter than she should have for a simple training session before letting go.

And then Jake felt his knees wobble as his body weaved back and forth, side to side, as if he truly were riding the waves. He carved in place, extending his forearms to help, but he couldn't hold for long and found that it wasn't as easy to switch up like he was on a skateboard. The only thing being carved up now, as he hurtled towards the ground, would be his elbows.

"Ker-splat," intoned Cameron as she helped him back up.

"That bad, huh?" Jake asked, breathless. He could feel the heat pulsating in his ears with the same rhythm as his heart. He couldn't remember the last time he'd worked this hard while practicing his surf skills.

But the ache he felt in his paw-pads, knees, and elbows was almost negligible, compared to the good time he was having trying and failing with this.

Most of all, it was the good time he was having with Cameron.

"You need to relax your body, Jake," Cameron instructed. "Loosen up, you're way too stiff."

"I thought I was loose," the Labrador replied, wriggling his forelimbs like noodles.

"Not like that you're not. Do you even exercise regularly when you're watching those bad horror movies?"

"Does reaching for potato chips count?"

Cameron smirked. "Only if you want to get sciatica or bust up your internal rotators. Sit on the ground, Surfer Boy. Let this cat teach you a few things."

Once Jake did as he was told, Cameron went right to work. She sat down behind him, mindful of his tail and extended his legs out front. "Keep loose and don't resist," she said, crossing his right leg over his left and placing his right foot flat on the floor, his right paw at rest against her thigh. Then she stretched his left arm and twisted his trunk and torso to the right.

"This is called the piriformis stretch," Cameron explained. "It's designed to work out your hips, back, ass. You know, all the stuff you're gonna need while surfing. You feel anything yet?"

Jake felt something, alright: between his back cracking like a sawed-in tree ready to collapse, he began to feel his cock continue its long and slow inflation inside his thin shorts. The tautness and the pulsation of the veins, it had to be as a result of being this close to Cameron and feeling the soft fluff of her body against his, and the radiating heat which seemed to waft from her chest to his back.

She was resting her head on his shoulder as she shifted positions, voice dropping slightly lower as she continued to issue instructions. Cameron was all business, making sure he was breathing and twisting with each lunge as she bent and straightened his body on that court.

Then she giggled lightly, and said, "You know, I've never

done this with anyone else. You're my first, just so you know."

"Y-yeah?" he managed to squeak and gazed into Cameron's lime-colored eyes. His imagination wasn't lost on the fact that her paws brushed dangerously to his growth as she maneuvered his hips here and there, bending and splaying and rubbing if she felt the heat growing along his muscles, always making sure he was good and loose. Twice the knuckles of one paw touched against his cock and it sprung to life in response, the blood coursing with a fiery rage he could barely contain by thinking about baseball cards.

Jake hoped that they would finish soon. There were public showers he could dip into and jack off to his heart's content.

For Crike's sakes I don't think I can last like this, he thought ruefully. He didn't want to think about the last time his other muscle had been worked out with something that wasn't his paw. *But I wonder how her paw would feel wrapped round my shaft. She's* definitely *got the strength!*

"Hey, you okay there?" Cameron asked. "You went radio silent on me."

"F-fine," Jake sputtered. "Just...doing fine."

"Good. Oh hey, there's Gina coming down to check on us. She's the one who taught me my moves."

"Is...is that right?" Jake asked, just as Gina walked over towards them.

The red squirrel was still dressed in her tightly fitting swimsuit, hugging into her thick thighs and large breasts. Her bushy tail bounced high behind her, and an anklet rattled against her talus. Once more, a fiery wave of lust burned from Jake's heart down to his loins as he tried not look at the thinly concealed cleavage. How many times had he seen that same squirrel peeled from her uniform?

Too many, and he was grateful for the fact that his shorts were black, hiding the likely spreading patch of precum trickling from the cocktip.

"Hey, you look happy to see me, Jake," Gina quipped.

"What's that supposed to mean?" the Labrador asked.

"Oh, you know, I see Cam there showing some of her

stretches. Figuring she's probably taught you some stuff."

"And how!" Jake said, already feeling some of the soreness creep into his now cooling muscles.

"You two know each other?" Cameron asked.

"Since high school," confirmed Gina. "Getting this dork to exercise is a miracle, but he seems to be learning pretty good. How's your hearing today, Cam?"

"Pretty good, though I wish they'd make an aide that was waterproof," she replied. "Though this is pretty fun, working with him. He's getting pretty good already!" Then, blushing deeply inside the pink of her ears, she hinted, "But you're always the best," and moved towards Gina.

It was at first a hug as the Rex threw her arms around the taller squirrel, with Gina lifting Cameron off her feet. Once back on the ground, the two gazed in each other's eyes and there appeared a magnetic pull between them as their faces grew close and their lips pressed together.

Open mouths, their tongues twirled over one another while Jake watched and his heart pounded hard against his breast.

Gina...and Cameron.
Gina and Cameron.
Cameron...and Gina.
Of course.
Dammit.

It made sense now and he felt as embarrassed as he had earlier for not picking up the signals of Cameron's deafness. He considered leaving but the longer their kiss lingered, with the pair lost in an air of intimacy that seemed to not be mindful of no one else but them, his gaze lengthened and so did his cock.

Finally, it was Cameron who broke away, giggling like a schoolgirl caught doing something naughty. Turning her attention back to Jake, she said, "Sorry about that! Now where were we?"

"Uh, still stretches," Jake said, paws dangling between the middle of his crotch in a pose of repose, concealing the rapid awakening of his member.

"Ah-ha! Here, let's get you into the Reclining Bound Angle

Pose."

"Oh that's my favorite!" Gina chirped. "Mind if I watch you, Jake?"

"N-not at all," Jake answered, and before he could get himself composed, Cameron had wrapped her forelimbs around his waist and leaned back, resting Jake's back on her stomach, his tail tucked between her legs. Her paws trailed down his sides and widened his legs, cupping around his thighs and it was all the canine could do to suppress the shivers coursing through his body at the softness of her touch.

Then, he heard the squeal behind his ears and felt her digits against the sides of his shaft. He watched Gina step closely and then cup her paws to her snout as she gasped.

Oh no, Jake shuddered in his mind, afraid to look down.

"Jake, why are you so *hard?*" Cameron asked. There was his erection, thick and veiny and twitching madly, standing out from between his shorts. He rolled from on top of Cameron and covered his middle quickly, blush rushing to his ears.

"Sorrysorrysorrysorry!" he said breathlessly as he ran back in the direction of his car, hopping in and barely waiting for the engine to spring to life before he pulled out and sped away. He burned through stoplights and did not breathe until he got home, and only then after he'd masturbated.

With his tail tucked between his legs, Jake slunk to the southern end of North Beach for a couple days afterwards. He'd stopped bringing his board and just sat in the dunes watching everyone else jump and play and splash and surf, though his eyes were in that typical half-moon expression of anxiety, licking his lips in depression.

It was better than going back to the main end and risk bumping into Cameron, let alone Gina. And as he walked along the dunes one late afternoon, he blamed himself for what had happened.

Maybe I can stay here for a while, he thought somberly at his obscurity. *No one seems to want to talk to anyone, and I think I can just disappear from Cameron's memory if I just sit right here and lie forgotten.*

The image of the Rex, however, was hard to push away from his memory. The mix of perfect athleticism and wry humor, the connection they developed and the way his own body had responded to her touches had been a cocktail he wished to partake of again, if he could have another chance. He even wondered how she was getting on with her hearing, if she was still cursing about her hearing aids not being waterproof. He hoped she was reading the signals better when her turn came around to take a wave.

Briefly he smirked, thinking of her tail slinking behind her ass, and that same ass bouncing to action as her knees bent to balance that lithe body of hers. The Labrador couldn't bring himself to think of her now as that cool, inattentive fellow surfer. She was someone that surfed the tides of his thoughts and likewise he regretted that she probably thought him a pervert now.

And just how the heck could he even think about competing with Gina? Usually the squirrel mentioned who her dates were, just in case something like this would ever happen. It ran the same way for him and kept things nice and orderly between their arrangement. How could she just "casually" forget to mention she was seeing Cameron?

Yet each night since that night, his dreams had grown to be quite arousing. Imagining Gina and Cameron—the ocean dripping from their fur, their round breasts freed from restrictive swimsuits, honey-spots completely soaked—sitting down on his middle and allowing nature to take its course...

Gotdammit. I'm getting hard again.

He squirmed and clamped his legs together, trying to hold back the stretches his dick was making inside his pants. Jake made a thought to go home, or at least get in his car and drive to the old bowling alley; there he could relieve his tension in privacy.

I've got a towel, and another pair of shorts back there. Yeah, think that's what I'll do. I'll just wait on this to settle down a little more and...

The thought was broken when he spotted a head bubbling up from the cool blue surface, spouting water like a whale. He thought at first that it was one of the swimmers here on the south end. Jake figured they must've swam up while he was feeling sorry for himself, until he narrowed his eyes to try and make something out of the blurry shape.

He could see by the pointed ears and shape of the long tail curling behind that it was a feline of some sort, and the more he squinted, he could see the chocolate brown fur coat and the little white spots along the thighs. But it wasn't until the figure had fully stepped out of the ocean's roar and approached the shore that her scent was carried in the breeze, with his heart pumping so hard fast that it might have burst from his chest in red fury.

It was Cameron. And when she approached the dunes where Jake sat, he felt his breath leave him. She flashed him a quick smile, then hesitated upon seeing the bewildered look on his face. Then she relaxed a little after seeing the transparency of his gaze along her body for she wore a thin green bikini, giving Jake a good view of all the areas that would push his erotic buttons.

Crikes she's really pretty, Jake thought when she walked up to him. He could make out the shape of her gentle breasts, with their dark pink areolae surround her lighter pink prominent nipples. His eyes then traveled down to her center and saw how low the crotch of the bikini's bottom revealed her finely trimmed mound, briefly illuminated by the still glistening sea which clung tight to it.

She looked down and he looked up. Neither said anything for a while, letting the song of the gulls fill the gulf of that uncomfortable silence. Then, Cameron sat down next to him, looking at the Labrador as he felt his ears once more fill hotly with blush.

"Look," Jake said, turning his head away from her. "I'm sorry about the other day."

He paused, waiting on a response.

Nothing.

Dammit she must be pissed at me still.

"I didn't mean to get all...you know. You know...it just happens. I guess I wanted to say that it happens kinda randomly, but well...you know. On top of that, I didn't imagine you and

Gina being you and Gina, so that was a shocker. So I'm sorry if I messed something up there with you two..."

Jake paused again and waited patiently to be screamed at. He turned back towards Cameron to see her looking at him.

Instead of a stern expression or of massive disappointment, it was one of confusion. Then she pointed towards her ears and shook her head, holding out her paws at the same time.

Then he remembered and threw up his paws in frustration. *Of course she doesn't have her hearing aids in if she swam here.*

The Rex held up her forepaw and then drew in the sand: *"If it's about the other day, it's okay."*

She smiled and looked back at Jake as he read the message. He then turned his gaze back to hers and flashed a grin.

The canine followed and wrote his reply: *"I'm still really sorry. I'm not a pervert. REALLY!"*

Cameron laughed upon reading his response and Jake joined her.

Then, Jake added: *"I really like you and I want to kiss you."*

Her ears filling with hot red blush after she read, Cameron erased her previous message and added a new one in its place: *"I really like you too. And I want to kiss you too."*

Just as it had been when she had kissed Gina, Cameron's head gravitated towards Jake's slowly. The Labrador did not resist the dynamic pull, tilting his head until his muzzle met her snout and their lips were gently pressed together. Five seconds later it grew into a deeper osculation, filled with heavy breathing and moaning from the pair as their tongues waltzed inside each other's mouths. Neither was sure just how long it exactly lasted. When they finally did separate, both were smiling.

"That was amazing," wrote Cameron.

"Do you want to do it again?" Jake wrote in the reply. Cameron nodded enthusiastically, her ears forward as Jake snaked his arms around her and pulled her in close until their lips touched once more. This second embrace lasted longer than the first, their chests pressed together so that their hearts beat with a similar furor.

The intensity of that kiss had brought back his growing

member; he was now threatening to burst out of his shorts, and likened its resemblance to that of a pitched tent. The feline, ears blushing harder with her nipples standing on end through her top, now ran a paw up and down the lumpy threads of his cock's veins. She gripped his shaft tightly and stroked. Beads of precum bubbled through the fabric and a faint patch of wetness spread across the crotch of Jake's shorts.

She was quiet, ruminating over Jake's meat, her breath hard and heavy. He matched it himself, his heart beating faster as he attempted to rein in the waves of lust crashing through him like the sea lashing rocks. He leaned back on the dune and, with Cameron's gaze following, lifted his paw towards her abdomen then slid down low beneath her bikini bottoms.

A shiver of pleasure passed through the cat and she closed her eyes. *She's already so wet*, Jake thought, spreading her thighs for a better opening. She opened her eyes again, looking at him and increasing her strokes along his swelling cock, now freed from the cell of his shorts, the undulating vibrations both felt passed from one to the other. Jake teased her hardening clitoris between his digits, and her body responded kindly by moistening his palm. In turn, Cameron's paw worked his sheath like a machine, melting all sense and place from Jake's brain.

"I bet this is the kind of thing you've whacked off to the last few days."

Jake was brought back into reality and looked up at the source of the new voice. It was Gina, cutting into the moment like a knife through butter. She was standing above Jake and Cameron, startling the Labrador so much he almost came right then. The red squirrel was fully nude: where her russet tawny pelt dissolved into ivory were her breasts, the pink nipples poking through her white chest fur. Jake's gaze trailed down her abdomen until they fell on her slit. Already it was glistening with excitement as she sashayed her curvy rear towards the pair.

Jake made a motion to start to his feet, pulling his shorts back up. But it was Cameron who laid a gentle paw on his chest and eased him back into his reclining position. Despite the interruption, the excitement had failed to deflate him, much to the pleasing gleam in Gina's eye.

"In case you're wondering, this is all Cam's idea," Gina said, wrapping her paw around Jake's cock. She moved slow and worked the tip, getting her left paw gooey with Jake's precum. "Gotta say, she definitely has good taste in partners. When I told her just who it was that saved her, you should've seen the way her heart melted. She'd seen you plenty before, but never really knew how talk to you without it becoming awkward. I told her you were the King Dork of Awkwardness so it'd be no problem at all."

Jake could barely speak. Cameron was now standing and had dropped her bottoms to the ground. Stepping out of them, she glided back towards Jake and Gina and got down on her knees. The Rex looked to Gina and an exchange was shared between them, one that made Jake tilt his head with one ear raised.

"What're..." Jake began, but the words never made it past his maw as Cameron took his cock and placed it in her mouth. The erection returned, the feeling of Cameron's tongue swirling around his member lusciously and violently as she bobbed her head up and dead. The veins grazed against the edges of her mouth while Gina worked the sac and leaned up towards Jake, gazing long and furtively at him, the digits of a paw dancing and teasing the tender skin underneath.

"I don't know why you're pretending to be confused," Gina said, rubbing Jake's sac. "Just a few minutes ago you seemed *really* happy to see Cam, and I'm going to trust that you're just as happy to see me too." Tilting him just slightly to the side, Gina gave the canine a view of her paws working at her moistened hearth, parting the labia and slipping the digits of a paw inside.

"When I told her about you, and me, and you and me," Gina began, breathing deep, "well, you can imagine the quandary that put the poor girl in. She likes you, you like her. She likes me, I like her, and I like you both. So how do you think we solve this problem?"

Jake thought he said something clever, as if he were in a late-night Cinemax softcore. But all the XXX-rated movies in the world could not prepare him for the mush that his brain had become, as he lost the ability to form a cohesive sentence and instead a moan escaped from his mouth.

The squirrel and the cat worked their mouths along the sides of Jake's cock, with Gina kneading the tip of the head into her paw. Mentally, Jake was tensed while his body went rigid, hanging back the deep epochs of desire building inside. He was hardened to a point—he doubted that rigidity could be broken, so much like iron it was.

Both girls took turns in swallowing and sucking on him, taking him as far as they could both go before realizing their limitations. Plunging up and down and sucking along the length of his cock, they appeared to work in sync with one another without a word being spoken between them. It was just a blink and a nod, or a gesture of the paw, and Cameron would run her rough tongue along the uppermost fleshy area of Jake's dick followed by Gina licking and tasting him underneath.

Neither let up in their oral attack, and when Gina glanced up to Jake's eyes and saw only seconds were left before the eruption, she got Cameron's attention to get ready. Both fixed their mouths together over his cockhead just as Jake exploded, shooting stream after stream of his jism deep down their waiting throats.

Left limp, the Labrador collapsed back onto the dune and breathed deep, while Gina and Cameron cleaned the edges of their mouths from the bit of protein Jake had given them. With some of Jake's release still dribbling from the corners of Gina's lips, Cameron went over and licked her partner clean, which led to a passionate kiss and exchange of Jake's load between them and swallowed.

"Don't think you're going to get out of this that easy!" Gina effused. "You still with us, Jakey?"

Still lost in his post-orgasmic bliss, Jake mumbled something as he watched Gina stand up and then stand over his head, giving the canine an up close view of her sopping wet cunt. She licked her lips then dove in towards Jake's head, kissing him and letting him taste himself off her. The squirrel made a gesture towards Cameron, who understood as she crawled over Jake's crotch and seemed to hang there, eyeing both the squirrel and the canine.

"She's waiting for you to give the okay," Gina panted to Jake. "She told me that she doesn't want to go all the way if we all can't be in agreement."

He lifted his eyes to the want and desire radiating from the cat. This was like what she had talked about the other day. The stuff about just "feeling" something, even if you couldn't hear it. It wasn't just about sounds, but just having the entirety of your body in tune with the vibrations around you to feel them. To surf those vibrations, could he stay afloat?

Could he make this thing—whatever was happening—a reality?

Cameron managed a smile, as if she was telling him to relax and let things be.

And so, Jake did. He nodded to both Cameron and Gina.

"Good," Gina replied, easing her sweet spot down on Jake's waiting tongue. She let loose a deep, sensuous breath as his mouth touched her labia. "Me and Cam...we hoped you would." The squirrel let out a squeal of glee while Jake's tongue slid deep inside her, parting her labia and licking her already moistened walls like a bumblebee collecting nectar.

That had always been something Jake knew Gina liked, as he attempted to reach inside to the very ends of her slit and worked her quivering clit side to side. He pressed his lips hard across her labia folds up to her clit, orally venerating what had always been one of his favorite ways to pleasure the squirrel as she grasped his head and expressed the tension coursing through her body. Murmurs and vibrations followed, creating waves of sonic pleasure.

Cameron made a decision, having looked down at Jake and felt the same pangs of want. No, she *needed* what Gina was having done to her by Jake. Having never seen anyone of that size ever, just that taste—with its mix of sweet and salty—had been like an elixir transforming something inside of her.

She wanted more of that.

And she needed more of Gina and Jake.

Cameron lingered over the tip of Jake's half-sleeping

member. She then slid a paw down to feel him, and it was a few quick strokes to wake him back up. Ears filling full of blush, she took his dick and massaged the entrance until the head was just at the tip of her hole, and eased herself down, not moving as she made herself comfortable. But the warm feeling of having Jake inside of her quickly spread and she was soon moving her hips to the pulsating rhythm of Jake's throbbing member. She arched her back and threw her head high to the sun, moaning hard and even screaming to the sky at the occurrences stirring in her.

"*Oh...my...gosssshhhh!*" she wailed, with a clarity that made Gina and Jake pause momentarily to marvel at. As Gina stepped away from Jake's face, the canine shot out his arms and held the cat at her lower back, her tail curling in ecstasy as he pulled her forward and wrapped his mouth around those pinked nipples, while Gina took the other, dancing her own long tongue around Cameron's areola which quivered inside of her mouth.

Jake rocked his own hips in and out of Cameron, his dick tripling with each thrust and her cunt receptive. No words were passed; it was all through feeling and moments, as Cameron took Jake's head and once more kissed him with a ravenous passion, bodies writhing as Gina kissed the cat's neck and played with her breasts, teasing those nipples until she could feel Cameron's spine tense up as the prelude to her orgasm.

Trembling as the surging hurricane of that release poured from Cameron, Gina slid Jake's cock out of the cat and licked at her still sensitive slit, precipitating an encore while at the same time keeping Jake hard and ready.

"I hope you've got enough left in you to give me some," Gina cooed, worshipping the canine's length. She kissed Jake, then brought Cameron's head towards them both, lips and tongues waltzing and twirling with one another as Jake too felt the sopping wet nectar which dripped from both girls' hearths.

They laid back in the middle of the blanket, cuddling and kissing one another, sharing not many words except the deep and pleasing moans of satisfaction, appreciation, and love. Gina rolled to her side, back facing Jake, as Cameron helped him enter her. The squirrel shivered, she had forgotten just exactly how *big*

Jake was, and a deep moan escaped from her until Cameron provided a ministration by rubbing her clit and Jake proceeded to fuck her in the way he knew she liked. He almost let himself go completely there, feeling himself crushed between her powerful thighs. He'd just barely managed to crawl back from the edge with all the serious motions of heavy breathing he could muster.

And then it was Cameron's turn, as she rolled over to take Jake inside. But Gina gripped his dick and shared a look with him, pointing the head to her backdoor. Mischievously, Gina took her moistened digit and slid it first inside the cat's ass, testing it to hers, Jake's, and quickly Cameron's approval once she realized what was about to happen back there. The head teased at the pucker of her relaxed asshole, until it grew tired of knocking and let Jake inside.

Jake was still solid when he slipped into Cameron's ass, while Gina held their wriggling partner as she gasped at the lightning bolts of pleasure shooting through every inch of her body. Cameron craned her head and searched for Gina's lips, meeting her as wave upon wave of orgasmic electricity destroyed all other thoughts as Jake kissed at the nape of Gina's neck. At the same time, Cameron squeezed down on Jake's cock—the concentration was broken and with one final trembling moan he lost it, shooting wave upon wave of his jizz inside of the cat to the brim, which overflowed like a saucer of milk.

When the devastating string of orgasms between the trio ceased, they had all collapsed in a heaving, warm heap among each other. They were snuggled up and spooning closely, with Gina and Jake on one side and Cameron in the middle, all gently playing with another's sticky fur from that day's lust. And yet, there was no urgency for another round, just the wordless enjoyment of a lover's embrace.

Jake's eyes fluttered open, as he realized he was gazing on the setting sun. He looked to both girls and kissed them both between their ears. Gina was lost in her own bliss but Cameron stirred, and met Jake's gaze, smiling and spent.

"I won't be able to hear you if you say something," Cameron

began, "so I'll just say it all and you can tell me your thoughts when I get my hearing aids in."

Jake nodded for her to continue.

"I don't want to keep fucking nonstop, Jake. I mean, I like the fucking—good grief you're both good!—and I like you and Gina both, but I want us to try and work together as...something. Whatever this is that just happened, it's made me more happy than a perfect day on the waves. And I want there to be a next time, between all of us."

That "next time" was far from casual, and it was enough to send a joyous shiver down Jake's body and awaken his dick from its well deserved rest. He could feel it radiate from her too, as red blush rose to her ears and she looked down bashfully. Jake reached over and lifted her head back up, meeting her with a soft kiss.

Cameron then signed the words, "I love you," making the heart shape towards Jake and Gina, which Jake quickly picked up on as he caressed the bit of fur which stuck up between her ears. He smiled and his tail wagged happily

"You two lovebirds better save some for me next time if we're doing this officially," Gina quipped, not opening her eyes.

He wanted there to be a next time too and Jake wordlessly agreed.

"I'm glad. But til then, we all can't go home covered like this!"

Jake was prepared to ask what she meant, but had barely gotten the words out when Gina grabbed him and Cameron by their paws towards the wild surf, the cat and canine both flashing grins to the other and then at Gina. The trio all fell into a modest wave as their nude bodies wrapped around one another in a submerging embrace, letting another current surge them back towards shore.

That's the Thing with Love

Patrick D. Lambert

"Ok, now smile."

The tiger tried to simulate a charming smile, holding a thumb up. But his lips trembled, and the visible fangs gave him an eerie appearance. His younger counterpart put down the cellphone and frowned.

"Dad, it's a profile pic, not your mugshot from Discovery Investigations."

The old tiger shrugged and let out a long sigh of defeat. "This is dumb."

"C'mon, just relax! Think about something funny." He paused and looked down, hand on his chin. His father couldn't stop seeing his younger self in that pose. Some seconds after, the young tiger snapped and glanced back at him. "I know! Remember when Kyle mistook the liquid soap from hair gel and you and mom spent the next hour rinsing his fur because he used a lot?"

Both of them laughed just as an even younger feline made it into the bedroom.

"Yeah, pretty funny. I'll make sure to tell your friends what you were doing with your pants down the last month," he threatened, carrying a stuffed backpack on his back. "Bet Cassie is gonna love that story."

"Oh, you don't wanna do that, cub!"

Daryl beamed at the sight of the two young felines playing around the sofa, laughing and calling each other nicknames while one tried to catch the other, as if nothing had changed. For better or for worse, they barely shared features from their mother, besides the black-spotted ears and the striped pattern on their tails; the rest was him when he had twelve and sixteen years respectively, from the golden fur to the green eyes, a painful reminder those two tigers were his children.

"Ok, ok, stop that, boys," he said, standing in between the joyful tigers. "I don't want your mom asking why you two spend the entire week arguing again."

"Blame Mr. Language for it," said the younger one, Kyle, escaping from his brother's grasp. "He's the one thinking we're always arguing."

"Yeah, I can't say fuck without feeling his breath on my neck," added Gerald before taking a look at his cellphone. "It's really weird. Mom's here."

"You shouldn't be saying that, actually," Daryl pointed out, not so sure about what he was saying.

"That's exactly what he says. And with the same voice. We hate it," Kyle took his backpack from the ground and walked towards the door.

"Just kidding," Gerald said, afraid his dad didn't notice the sarcasm in the cub's voice. He picked up his own backpack from the sofa. "We still don't get used to his attitude. He's not like..." he made a pause to ponder his comparison, "... it's still new for us."

"Gerald, hurry up. There's a slice of cake at home with my name on it."

"Go ahead. I'll catch up with you in a moment."

"And risk ourselves to another lecture about 'not leaving your little brother alone'? I'll pass."

Gerald cringed at the mention of it, looking back at his father before exaggerating a deep voice.

"There are a lot of people out there who could potentially hurt your brother. You should never, ever, leave him alone in a place none of you know."

Daryl held it for a moment, but he imagined the slender cheetah with sunglasses saying that, and he chuckled, covering his mouth with one hand. His son, victoriously, snapped a picture of him.

"Well, it doesn't say 'I'll skin you alive in my basement dressed as my mother', so it's a progress," he gave a fistbump at his father's shoulder and walked towards the door.

Following his children into the hallway, Daryl wished it was progress.

Daryl went on a search for old colleagues. His son Gerald instructed him how to use the search engine and the most important aspects of privacy. Within a couple of days, Daryl found some old friends from his frat and tried to keep a conversation with them. They were married, with children, a nice house, a SUV in the garage, and planning the next vacation to Florida. Some had a cheaper car or planned to visit a colder place, but all the rest was similar. And none of them could go out to have a beer, whether because they were busy at work or moved to another state.

He did enjoy talking with them and remembering all the stuff they did in their youth. And those memories acted as a spark for something he forgot about—or more like kept hidden for years.

Making sure to cover his tracks, the tiger started to look for something more... adequate to his tastes—if the site already recommended him date apps, he figured there were apps for something more direct. And he found one; he made his profile, took a look at some guys close to his apartment, and minutes later closed the app, feeling guilty about looking for something like that.

He did not uninstall it. It stayed on his phone, sending him a notification now and then from some weirdo who wanted pics of his paws or asked to spank him with a pallet. The few times he decided to try and contact someone he found cute, they either said nothing or told him he was too old for their tastes.

Then someone appeared. Under the profile's name of Oswald, the otter messaged him to praise how good he looked in his picture—the same one Gerald took. In his mid-twenties, the mammal in the picture wore a green bow tie and suspenders, and Daryl couldn't say if it was his daily attire or something he used for a costume party. The rest of his pictures had a certain demure, barely showing any fur compared to the carnival of sausages and peaches that was the entire app.

And he was nice to him. His profile didn't give much data to work with; the description alone worked perfectly to scare those looking for something quick without looking like a moron. And even when he was fully dressed, the mischievous stare and smile said he planned something a little more private.

Oswald lived not too far from him, in a small apartment with a nice view of a bunch of other apartments that had no notion of what curtains were. He loved *Star Wars* to death and wasted way too much time putting together Lego sets. No one had faith in him and his art degree till he started working in a gallery. And rum was his favorite beverage.

He was special in a way he couldn't explain. Daryl wanted to add him on Facebook after both agreed it was awkward to keep talking between ads of glorified Viagra pills and escorts offering a discrete service, but Oswald wanted to keep it all in the app, since his Facebook profile was entirely for his family. Weird, but he understood, considering what his kids would say. Still, he wanted to know him more and more, beyond the chat.

And when he invited him to a date, Oswald accepted in seconds.

The otter was free only during the weekends. Daryl tried to convince him, but Oswald couldn't due to his work. And the kids only visited him on weekends. He felt that crushing guilt again, keeping at every moment his cell phone next to him, pondering the idea of canceling. How selfish of him to put the kids aside to have a moment alone with someone he met on a dating app. What an awful dad he was. Then, when he tried to start the conversation that would probably be the last one, he imagined the otter's smile and laugh, and craved that touch from another living being, and he couldn't do it.

On Friday night, sitting at the edge of his bed, Oswald messaged him to confirm: "Ready for tomorrow, gramps? Those cheesecakes are gonna blow your mind."

"Hey... umm, I don't think I can go...."

"C'mon, do you think I'm gonna ditch you? I waited soooooo long for you to invite me."

"It's not because of that."

"I didn't say something about myself. And I don't wanna say it now because it might scare you."

"What? Are you a very tall midget? Or do you have a fetish with midgets? Because I'm really open about that stuff."

"Don't be silly...."

He couldn't write it immediately. How dumb he felt with his hands sweaty and trembling like a teenager wanting to confess his feelings. How dumb he was for thinking he had a chance with someone like him. It was impossible.

"I'm divorced. My kids are coming to visit this weekend."

No answer for a while. He knew it was over. Oswald probably blocked him by that moment and moved to the next contact on his list. It was the—

"Got a really cool idea. Send me your address. I promise you're gonna love it."

He stared at his cell phone for a moment. None of that seemed real, and he re-read the words several times believing he read it wrong. But the words were there, real as the heart pumping hard inside his chest. Daryl swallowed. He placed the phone on the bed, walked across the room, looked back at the phone, and walked again, more anxious with every step. Trust him? A complete stranger? And not only that, but a stranger he met on an gay dating app! Trust him and let him come into his house while his kids were around? He wasn't that stupid. He wouldn't fall for something like that...

...but he wanted to see him. He had been dreaming of him and wanted to see that smile in person.

And he was so, so lonely.

Saturday morning. Gerald and Kyle shared a dazzled expression after seeing Dad sitting on the coffee table, interrupting the show they were watching. The tiger cleared his throat and began the speech he practiced early in the morning.

He babbled the words, seeing the fur from his arms turning whiter.

"So... I invited someone today. He's a friend of mine. We are gonna chat. There," he pointed at the dinner table behind the kids.

Kyle tilted his head. But Gerald smiled with confidence and pride.

"Sure. I can take Kyle to the room if you want."

"But the bedroom TV is smaller," the cub protested, already puffing his cheeks to make a tantrum.

"I'll lend you my laptop to play, sounds good?"

Bargain accepted.

"No need for that, kids. You can stay here, we're just gonna talk. I don't think he's gonna—"

The doorbell interrupted him. For Daryl, it felt like standing beside the biggest bell in the world. He fell from the coffee table, pushing it back. It made him forget completely what Kyle did when someone called, and only after the cub jumped from his seat to run towards the door his brain decided to retake the most basic functions.

"I'll get it!" Kyle announced.

"There's no need for that, son!" Daryl ran to reach his son, getting there just in time for him to open the door.

On the other side, a juvenile otter stood, his eyes jumping back and forth between both felines. He looked just like his pictures, with his clothes only having a more brighter tone. Face to face, he reached the tiger's pecs, barely, which put him at the same height as Gerald. He gave Daryl a warm smile before kneeling to face the little Kyle.

"And who's this handsome fella?"

"My name's Kyle. Who are you?" the cub giggled, holding the trembling hand of his father.

"I'm Oswald. I'm a friend of your father. He told me to come today."

"W-wasn't expecting you this early," he barely managed to put the words together, failing in an attempt to look calm.

"Well, had a lot of free time already. Might at least give it a good use."

He was beautiful. More than anyone he has seen before. There was a gleam in his eyes that gave him hope, the sort of look you find in someone who has no fear of the unknown. He made him feel younger; it was the same sensation as when he discovered his attraction to males. And the same urges to explore more.

"So, can I come in?"

"Sure! Sure!"

Oswald walked inside, looking around like a newcomer looking at a place he wanted to rent. He directed his attention to Gerald when he was closer to him.

The bigger tiger did something similar. The tip of his tail hooked to the right, barely moving.

"You two look a lot like your father, you know?"

"Yeah, we do," he smirked, now conscious of having the same height as the otter. "I'm Gerald."

"Nice to meet you, Gerald. Your dad talked a lot about you. I was really excited to meet you." He left his backpack over the chair next to him. "So excited I told him, 'You know? I wanna draw a picture of your lovely family,' and he said, 'That would be amazing! And I'll be more than happy to pay you two hundred dollars for it,' and who was I to say no to such noble gesture."

Daryl choked when he tried to reply. And Kyle was beyond the excitement he usually reserved for Christmas and his birthday. Like a bolt, he reached for the otter's arm and looked up at him, his eyes full of admiration.

"You're a painter?!"

"Yes, I am. Been drawing since I was a child."

He zoomed out in an instant and disappeared inside the guest room. Ten seconds later, he stumbled out carrying a really worn-out notebook in his hands.

"And we lost you," Gerald declared as soon as the cub stood in front of Oswald.

"I draw too! Here!"

Oswald took the notebook when Kyle offered it to him and started to look at every page. His surprise was genuine, as he had found more than the usual scribbles from a beginning artist.

"Wow, I wasn't expecting concept art."

"Do you like it?"

"It's not my area of expertise, but this is actually really good for someone of your age," he gave Daryl a quick look over the shoulder. "You know he has a future on this, right? Because I'm gonna hit you if you say no."

"I like creating new things," Kyle giggled, then immediately rubbed his left arm, "but I'm not good at making people."

"That's fine. What you're doing here is pretty good too! I might show it to a friend that knows more about the topic, and meanwhile give you some tips if you want."

"That would be amazing!" Kyle exclaimed, already jumping in place.

"Kyle, he came to visit dad," Gerald pointed out to no avail, his brother too excited to listen.

"Don't worry. I should have imagined this would happen." Daryl followed his game, getting closer to the otter. He felt so small at his side. "I mean, I don't care as long as you don't."

"I wish I had someone to teach me when I was his age." Oswald took the closest unoccupied chair, and Kyle rushed to the one in front of him. "Instead, I dealt with my parents telling me it was a waste of time. Dad even said I would end up living on the streets. Can you believe that?"

"I... I think I can."

The tiger took the chair in between, glad Oswald didn't notice his expression. The otter quickly pulled out of his backpack a pen and paper and started to explain concepts and things that were out of his range of knowledge, but that his young child understood with no trouble.

It was something worth watching. Daryl couldn't remember the last time Kyle focused so much on someone. He was the kind of child whose attention jumped back and forth between everything. And that otter managed to keep him listening to everything he said. It was such a rare sight that even Gerald joined for a moment before going to his room to start his homework.

He had a way with words, Oswald. It was a skill not limited to how he expressed himself through chatting, but Daryl noticed how good the otter was linking word after word to make a speech no one would dare to ignore. And then there was his smile. And his eyes. And how he leaned the head to the left when he asked something. You couldn't just ignore someone that... what was the word Gerald used the other day?

"Wholesome...."

"Hmm, did you say something?"

Daryl snapped. He was lost in thoughts he didn't notice how fixated his look was on the otter. Or how loud his thoughts were.

"No, just thinking about work. Sorry."

"Work, sure," he chuckled, then went back to the cub. "That should be enough for one class. We can schedule another one, but I gotta talk with your dad first about it."

"I know he's gonna say yes." Kyle took his notebook and went to the bedroom. "Gerald, look what Oswald teached me!"

"Of course you're gonna say yes. Otherwise I'll kick your ass into oblivion." The threat came with a joking tone.

"You're gonna do it before or after I pay you the two hundred?"

"Oh, that was a joke. My prices are higher, actually. Like, three times higher," he enjoyed seeing the tiger choke with his own saliva. "But you can take me to a fancy place for dinner sometime. Consider it the revenge for not telling me about your children."

"Sounds fair."

"So, now that we're alone"—he got up for a moment to model himself to the tiger, both arms up—"is it everything you wished for?"

"Might need to get rid of some clothes, but so far it's exactly what I hoped for."

"Everything in place, I can assure that," Oswald chuckled. His look took a sudden turn to a more serious tone. "Look, before we continue, there is something I wanna talk with you. And I wanna say it now because I want to be fully honest with you."

He was confused. The comment came so out of nowhere that he thought it was something about Kyle. But his face wasn't of someone who just said a white lie. Only then his insecurities came back, and an infinite amount of scenarios crossed his mind, with Oswald leaving in every one of them.

"I only ask for you to listen. If I finish and you want me to leave, I'll do it."

"What could be... so serious to say that?"

"I wouldn't say it's serious, but it might not be something you want." He made a pause. "I am in a relationship with someone else. We've been dating for the past four years. And before you ask, I am not cheating on him. He knows that I'm here, he knows what I want with you, and he is okay with it." And then he added quickly, trying a more relaxed tone, "He actually replied some of your messages when I wasn't around. He says you're a cool guy."

Someone else? Of course there was someone else. He was such a cute and handsome guy that was impossible he was single. But then, why was he there?

"It's not that he wants me to cheat on him either—because we know some people have a thing for that—nor are we in a fully open relationship. We just... love more than one person. I don't know how familiar you are with the term 'polyamory.'"

"... you love polygons?"

It was the otter's turn to feel confused. He frowned and seemingly pondered what Daryl just said. Then, covered his mouth to stop himself from laughing.

"You're such a dork! How could I not like someone like you? Because... I do like you. And I want to find out if I can feel more than that. Because I don't see why I shouldn't. I respect that most people choose a monogamous relationship, and I don't mind being in one, but just because I feel love for someone else doesn't make what I have with my boyfriend worth less. After all, they're always saying we should share our love with everyone—why does it have to stop when it's a romantic love? It doesn't make sense to me."

Then he continued.

"So I'm being honest here when I say that I like you. Truth is, I just wanted to get some hot pics from you, maybe a video and talk about naughty stuff; that's basically what I do on the app. But then you started to talk about your work and your dreams and how you always forgot the tea you prepared... and something clicked. Suddenly, all I wanted was to see you. And I wanted to say it in person, so you could see that I am interested in you and wasn't just making an elaborate lie to get rid of you. But if you're not fine with that, we can end it here and make as if nothing happened. Or just be friends, I don't know."

Daryl looked down.

"It's... it's too much to process."

And it was. Suddenly the guy he liked was in another relationship that wasn't exactly a relationship but worked the same way with the difference that he loved other people too. And it felt wrong for him in so many ways, being educated under the figure of marriage and carrying the mistakes of curiosity on his back.

"I just... how do I know you're not playing with me?"

"I can't prove it. You're gonna have to believe that."

Of course he couldn't. Even in a normal relationship there is no way to prove you can trust the other person. You have to do it. But this was no normal relationship. Not only did he have to put his trust in Oswald, but also in his boyfriend. How does that work? Did he have to trust one more than the other?

No, that wouldn't be trust.

"Why couldn't you have just told me that from the beginning?" He held his head with both hands, fearing it would fall off of his neck.

"I told you, I wasn't expecting to feel something for you. And I don't put it on my description because all those fuckers that are ok with sleeping and cheating suddenly became advocates for marriage and purity, telling me that all I want is to cheat on my boyfriend and not commit. Because that's what some people think about polyamory. And I'm tired of dealing with that. I just wanna let people I trust to know that part of my life. And I trust you enough to share it with you. Because I want to invite you on a date, and hold hands with you, and kiss you on the cheek, and send you corny stuff every morning." He made a pause, taking Daryl's hands between his. "I want to see where this leads, but only if you want."

Daryl moved his hands apart, much to Oswald's sadness.

"I don't know what to think."

Oswald waited for the tiger to continue, but the way his lips trembled and the look of defeat on his face told them everything he needed.

"It's okay. We can still be friends."

"I'm not saying I don't want to be with you, I just... this doesn't feel right for him. For your boyfriend."

"You can always talk with him. He wants to meet you. And he'll be happy to let you know this is okay for him too." Then he added, "We can go slower. You choose the pace. Till you're comfortable with this."

Till he's comfortable. Oswald made it sound as if it was something completely normal. And it was normal for him.

He was the one feeling love for more than one person. And it was okay for him.

But it wasn't for Daryl.

"I cheated on her." The words came out of nowhere, and only after noticing the confused and worried look on Oswald's face, Daryl rushed to explain. "Not sexually. I-I was talking with someone else. Someone from work. I had my experiences back in college, but took it as a phase. I met her. We married. I moved on."

"Until someone made you feel that again."

"Nothing happened. We just enjoyed each other's company. I thought of him as a friend and nothing more." His memory brought a smile to his face, one that he forgot he could show off. "But I was wrong. And when I noticed, it was too late. And she knew there was something wrong, and I couldn't hide it forever. So I did the cruelest thing and broke every dream she had in an instant." With tears crowding in his eyes, Daryl looked at the otter, who shared the same sorrow he felt.

"You were honest with her. That's more than what a lot of

people can do. You didn't cheat on her."

"I ruined everything!"

"You didn't. I don't know how things are going on with her, but I can bet my entire career that you are a great father. And I don't need to know them deeply to notice that. The way they talk and act and see you, and the interest you have for what they like—hell, I wish I had a father like that!"

A compliment was the last thing he expected, and it took him so much by surprise that even his cheeks burned under the fur.

"I'm not gonna let you blame yourself for something that happened years ago. I guess you're scared of going through something similar and causing trouble between me and Terrence, but that's not gonna happen because this is something that we both want. And if I am looking for this with you in particular, it's because he agreed. He wouldn't have accepted if he had the tiniest pinch of doubt. And I'm glad to see that you actually care for me. At most you reassured that I put my trust in someone worth it."

Daryl quickly wiped away the tears. It was hard to believe in what Oswald had said, but seeing the otter's eyes told him he wasn't lying.

"Do you mind if we go slower?" he finally dared to ask.

Oswald shrugged, now crying alongside him, and nodded.

What followed was something... weird. A couple of days later, Daryl received a message from an unknown number from someone who presented himself as Terrence. It took him less than a second to know it was from Oswald's boyfriend. The tiger avoided answering for the rest of the day, and it wasn't till that night that he gained the courage to take up the conversation.

A middle-age crocodile, Terrence was a different person compared to Oswald. With a lot of formality involved, the reptile talked about himself to help Daryl feel less awkward. He had been working on his own law firm for the last year, motivated by the otter as a way to have more control over his work—which implied having more work than before, but at least the kind he wanted.

To keep himself relaxed, he played tennis with some friends from his previous work. Given how little Daryl knew about it, Terrence took his time explaining it for him after the tiger declined an invitation to play. The idea of playing, though, started to gain terrain in Daryl's mind, who considered it was time to lose some weight.

He was an adult, after all. They both were adults. They didn't share the explosive and charismatic attitude from Oswald, so their conversations took a more friendly route, like old friends from college who wanted to get to know what has happened in their lives after all those years. And honestly? That made Daryl happy. That kind of friendship he never had with the rest of his coworkers, after so badly neglecting his social life since the divorce. After adding him on Facebook, and going through his pictures with friends and with Oswald—having a dinner, relaxing after a game, going on vacation—the tiger started to picture himself alongside the couple, laughing, smiling, being closer and closer, and the image wasn't as uncomfortable as it had been at the beginning.

On the other side, his flirting with Oswald continued. The otter gave lessons to Kyle during the morning, and at the evening they watched a movie—alone at first, then accompanied by the kids later. It turned easier as time passed by. Daryl took his hand and kissed him in public more often, and cuddled for longer periods of time when they were in bed. No one made a mention about the way Daryl smiled, nor of how often he started to post more pictures of himself, much to Gerald's surprise.

"If I knew it would take an otter to make you smile like that I would have presented you with the neighbor," he joked during one dinner, to which Daryl replied by hiding his face in shame and Oswald by laughing for a couple of minutes.

But there he was, falling deeper in love with him. From the sound of his voice to the way he trembled when he scratched his back, and the cute sounds he made after poking his belly. He never thought possible to feel so comfortable again. But after several dates and months later, there he was. Being happy again.

Then, both said the same thing, the same day. "I think it's

time to meet." And Daryl went back to point A.

"Everything is gonna be fine!"

"It's easier for you to say it considering you've been living together."

"You're just making a storm in a teacup. He's been dying to meet you. Even bought you your own tennis racket. Can't remember the last time I saw him that excited."

Daryl was about to explode since he left his apartment, just thinking all the possible worst scenarios for that dinner. But Oswald's comment stopped his paranoia for a moment, and he finally considered—even for a second—that Terrence was as nervous as him. They would meet in person for the first time, after all.

"Sounds like there had been others before me."

"Not too many. Well, not in a romantic way."

They stood before an enormous door in a massive hallway that stretched to infinity in Daryl's eyes. The doorbell played as a million bells inside his head. A giant walked forward, his steps made the ground shake. His heart skipped a beat. Tail curled. Claws about to retract. The knob turned around and....

A crocodile greeted both with open arms.

"Just the male I was looking for," he exclaimed.

Now Daryl felt dumb all dressed in total formality. Unlike him, the crocodile left the suit behind and wore just a slightly dirty tank top and short pants, giving a completely different vibe from the pictures in his profile.

"Come in, please." He went back into the apartment, followed by the couple. "Sorry for the look. I just can't stand being in a suit all week. So Oswald and I had the rule to wear the least possible clothes during the weekend."

"That's why I told you to ditch the suit," Oswald giggled and helped him with the suit, hoping that Daryl would be more comfortable without it. "I mean, you're not in a business meeting, dummy."

It felt more like the boyfriend meeting with the father for the first time. Despite the two years of difference, Terrence had the aspect of someone wiser—probably a quirk from his job. Taller, with more muscles, and while he offered him a friendly smile, the look of his face was of a male that wouldn't doubt to close his fangs around someone's neck when needed. A feral beast well hidden under the scales. He was someone from the opposite spectrum.

"Just relax and be yourself."

And the beast approached. His sharp claws closed around Daryl's hips. And he pulled him closer. The golden eyes shone, and his warm breath had a soft touch of liquor. It broke his guard. Being victim of such confidence was too much for the tiger to resist.

"You're as cute as he said, if not cuter."

"T-there must be some kind of misunderstanding," the tiger mumbled before Terrence pressed his snout against him.

"There isn't," Oswald said. "We will have dinner tonight. We just wanna taste the dessert first."

The otter stood behind him, undoing his pants. The crocodile started to undo one button after another from his shirt. A fantasy he never imagined developed right in front of him. And the only thing that came to his mind was to move aside.

"Time out! Time out!" he called, making a sign with his hands. "This is so flattering and everything, but it's kinda fast."

He took a moment to regain his breath, keeping a certain distance from the couple, who were now half-discussing their plan.

"I told you it was a bad idea."

"It went better inside my head."

"Let me take it from here, darling." Terrence adopted the diplomatic and serious look Daryl expected from the start. He took one step forward, keeping the distance between them. "Look, Daryl, we know this came out of nowhere. I'd be lying if I said I haven't been wanting to be intimate with you. We both want to. But I know you don't think of me the same you think of Oswald. And that's ok. It was the first thing I realized after he told me what he felt towards you. It was the first thing I realized after we started dating: that someone who wants to be with any of us might accept our relationship but won't share the feeling with both of us. And if that's the case between you and Oswald, it's fine. I won't forbid him the joy of being with you, because I have no right to do such a thing. It's his love, and he can share it with whoever he wants. And if I'm telling you this, it's because we know you're not the kind of person who would have sex purely for the sake of it. It must have meaning."

He stopped. Only then, Daryl noticed he was mere inches away from him, enough for the crocodile to hold his hands.

"You don't have to love me in order to love Oswald. I let him have that freedom. And I won't get mad if you wanna be in bed together—as long as you let me watch. But you already made it this far, and I know you wouldn't accept an invitation to dinner with the three of us alone if you didn't consider this might happen. Let me find what he sees in you, and I might fall in love with things he hasn't found in you."

Terrence lacked the sweet gestures of Oswald, but he knew his way with words, and Daryl found it hard to resist after what he just said. The reptile called him with a scratch under the chin, and when both maws were sealed in a kiss, Daryl melted between his arms as if from the taste of strong liquor.

It was nothing like the kisses he received from the otter. Sheer passion and lust. The real face of the beast living within. His fierce grasp kept him immobilized, and before he noticed, the small but skilled hands from Oswald made his way between the fur and muscles to get their clothes away.

Daryl couldn't resist any longer. The proximity of another male in a more intimate way, with no clothes in between and with their intentions clear from the very beginning. There was a special magic in a spontaneous encounter, the joy of not knowing what would happen next, having only lust as a guide.

And it told him to move on. He pulled apart from the crocodile and switched to the more delicate and tender otter, who didn't expect the ferocity now revealed by Daryl. More than a spark, it was an explosion that pushed the tiger. A mixture of his loneliness and desperation, of the solitude of a male driven by guilt, and the love and desire he so wanted to share with someone else.

The sharp fangs closed around his shoulder, and Daryl had to take a moment to moan. Loud. Oswald took his chance to take off the rest of his clothes now that his shirt was out of the way and his pants were waiting to fall down.

His bulge throbbed against his underwear. Two different hands groped it to play with it, following its shape across the fabric. It sent a shiver through his spine. He felt wanted once again—despite not seeing himself handsome or in shape, they enjoyed every inch of his body and his manhood.

With skilled manners the couple undressed, not stopping even for a second their devotion towards Daryl. Licking and biting from shoulders and neck, to his nipples and the sides of his belly. Their hands squeezed his thighs, and pulled down with a slow pace the tight and wet boxer, giving the tip of his shaft enough space to breath and feel the cold air from the room.

How much desperation a male could endure? He couldn't resist anything they did, and found himself being dragged to the bedroom between bites and licks and grips, leaving a trace of clothes in their wake.

"How does it feel?" Terrence murmured to his ear.

Daryl didn't dare to open his eyes, afraid it might break the spell he was under. Instead, he went right at the crocodile's neck. It was the first moan he made, with surprise mixed with pleasure. He pushed his luck and pressed his fangs a little more against the soft skin on his neck; he felt the sharp claws at his back, drawing traces in the fur as Terrence scratched it. Terrence might have been stronger, but Daryl found how to keep him under control after seeing how sensitive he was.

Below them, an eager otter went down on his knees and made space for both cocks to be free. One sharp shaft coming out of his slit, the other with a thick head and soft thorns covering it. The mixed musk pulled Oswald like a lasso, giving a quick sniff at them before putting his tongue to work. One lick to each shaft, going up and down, without neglecting his own throbbing and leaky manhood.

Slowly, gently, Daryl put him down in bed, until Terrence

broke free of his lusty grab and dragged himself up, leaving space for the otter to jump in. With his legs spread and Oswald rubbing his cock across his own face, the crocodile gave him for the first time the appearance of the dominant beast he was.

"Now, I bet you didn't have the pleasure of having two males for yourself." Fangs showing off as a challenge, Terrence pointed at the nightstand to his right with his look. "Grab the bottle of lube from there, stud. Unless you think it might be too much for you."

Anger was the natural response to his dare, but he took his physical condition in mind and felt a little scared about it. Years after the last time he slept with another male and he had the chance again with not one, but two handsome ones.

The drawer had all sort of provisions for an active lover: toys, rings, and a plethora of flavored lubes.

"Pick the green one. The mint-flavored one," Terrence suggested between moans, having Oswald blowing him off again.

"That's my favorite." The otter paused and added, "Feels cold at first, then hot as you start humping."

"Quite messy, too. Hope you don't have problems with tangled fur."

"Nothing a hot bath can't handle."

It was odd. Everything. Daryl had the idea of sex being special, intimate, a moment of peace and a silence only broken by the moans and verbal expressions of love. Yet they talked like discussing what spices go better with each food. It broke the fantasy he had for the night he finally had sex again, and it intimidated him at the same time. After all, he was clueless about sex. And those two apparently had it all the time.

The round cheeks of Oswald's ass wiggled a little after he waved his tail to attract the tiger. Impossible to resist to such a beautiful look, and his cock throbbed to second that motion. He poured the thick liquid over his shaft, then put some extra at the otter's hole, who gladly spread it for him.

"Don't worry about taking your time, kitty."

"Look for your own pleasure tonight. You deserve it."

His ass was soft to the touch. The size difference was finally obvious under that position; there was no way the slender frame of the otter would endure being between two giants. But he couldn't just stop at that point. It would be a blatant lie to say he hasn't been dreaming about having sex with Oswald. And after the tip of his cock felt his warm skin, everything else moved on its own.

The otter huffed, then moaned. He arched his back and grasped the crocodile's hands, which he offered as a support.

"F-forgot the head was thicker," he mentioned, his entire body wiggling with every inch going inside.

"Always chewing more than you can eat, hun." Terrence didn't hide the lust on his eyes, his visual enjoyment of seeing Daryl starting to move his hips forward and backward. "Don't worry too much, we're used to big sizes, but the real thing is something different."

But Daryl wasn't listening. The tiger was captivated by the torrent of sensations long forgotten. The tightness and warmness of a male's insides, the shape of his hips, how deeper and louder his sounds were. It was a completely different experience. He wanted to cum right away and just keep going till he finished again and again and again. The small part of his brain telling him to go slow melted under the intense lust, and all he could hear in his head was a roaring beast commanding him to go even faster.

"Didn't have to say it twice." Terrence smirked. He guided his boyfriend to retake the blowjob, and Oswald was more than happy to obey. Not just the crocodile was in heaven at that moment. "Good boy...."

There were no words for a long moment, only the sound of muffled moans, slurps and wet slaps. Three males leaving the manners behind and fucking like untamed animals. The musk was intoxicating, but for them, it worked to relieve the pain of a sore jaws and legs, pushing them to keep to, to satisfy their primal need.

The tiger was already drooling over his chest. A silly smile drawn in his face. Oswald already got used to the size, and Daryl felt comfortable with the pace, especially seeing the small otter moving his own hips to follow it. Such a dedicated bottom.

He wasn't the only one, though. Terrence raised his legs, and Oswald immediately knew what he wanted. A huge stud having his ass eaten by someone smaller was a blessed sight, and one he never dreamt of having a chance to enjoy. And there he was, a moaning crocodile being tongue-fucked by his boyfriend who had a tiger drilling deep into his ass.

"Love when you start doing the alphabet." Terrence curled his toes in clear ecstasy, much more submissive now.

"D-does it work as they say?" Daryl asked. He put one paw over the bed to get a better support.

"You gotta experience it for yourself."

Instinctively, Daryl made the letter with his own tongue, thinking he was the one rimming Terrence. He never did it in his youth, but seeing how much the crocodile was enjoying it caught his attention. His moans, his struggle, the submissive look on his face, he wanted to cause all of it and more.

He wanted to provoke it on both of them. A casual yet intimate moment that he knew both Terrence and Oswald wouldn't share with anyone else. But he was special. They saw him as someone special.

Daryl started to push Oswald forwards. His small body offered no resistance as he left his hubby's ass behind and climbed the chest till the couple ended up face to face, with Daryl now holding up the crocodile's legs. Never in his entire life crossed through his mind the idea of dominating someone, but there he was, having that first taste of control, absolutely sure the couple would follow his orders to the letter.

Oswald let out a moan after Daryl pulled out his shaft. Then Terrence flinched at the touch of the thick head.

"E-easy there, champ," he suggested.

It took him less effort—thanks to the rimjob—but he still found some resistance as he made his way inside the crocodile. A completely different sensation, way warmer than the otter. Sensitive too, judging by how his body jerked with every inch. Halfway in, he pulled out, then went back in, and Terrence shoved his claws into the sheets.

The pose was awkward and slightly uncomfortable, but he was too excited to stop at that moment. He kept the same pace, leaving his own pleasure aside for a moment to made sure Terrence enjoyed it as much as he was.

And he was. The crocodile smiled, all fangs showing up. It was as if he hadn't felt something like that in years. To provoke such sensations in someone else made Daryl feel much better with himself, with where he was and what he was doing. So he tried to do the same for both of them.

The crocodile let out a sigh when Daryl pulled out, and Oswald yipped a second after, feeling Daryl's shaft going in again. One minute of uninterrupted humping, then he went back into the crocodile, and repeated it at the same pace and for the same amount of time. It took the couple by surprise. Overpowered under that position, the only thing they could do was give up and let the tiger fuck them under his rules, jumping between both loosened-up holes.

"Wasn't expecting that..." Terrence managed to articulate, being the one with the cock inside him in that moment.

"You know I have a good eye for studs," Oswald replied, licking under the crocodile's chin.

It was exciting. A lot. And his body reacted to every single stimulus. The soreness in his thighs became more glaring, and his movements turned rougher and slower as he approached his climax. A tickling starting at the tip of his cock and quickly growing across his body. He couldn't hold it any longer.

A climax craved for so long, he pulled out his cock just in time for his load to shoot all over the couple, from Oswald's wiggling ass to the thick thighs of Terrence. His muscles tensed up. The orange fur bristled. And he moaned till he was breathless. It was an instant that lasted an eternity.

And just like that, he felt at their side, exhausted, sore, but satisfied. The couple admired him for a moment in silence, with a wide smile on their faces, before Oswald rolled in between the two giants and snuggled in Daryl's chest.

The otter felt asleep minutes after. It was the first time they were like that, with no clothes in between, and Daryl couldn't remember if he looked that handsome before.

"We're not gonna have dinner, right?" he finally dared to complain, being that the reason they invited him.

"Oh, there will be, just nothing too fancy."

He sighed. Everything seemed too fancy at that moment.

"What's gonna happen now?"

Terrence didn't reply immediately. Instead, he turned to lie on his side and face Daryl directly.

"Your choice. Oswald told me what happened with your marriage, and I understand if you're not comfortable with this. We can stop right here and just be friends, you and I. And you can continue what you have with him. He doesn't belong to me, nor does he belong to you, and it doesn't make the relationship he had with us less real. It's valid, as any other one. Because it's what we want."

"And if I want to stay?"

Terrence smiled and tried to get closer to kiss him once again, only to be interrupted by a groaning otter.

"You won't be staying for too long if you keep talking too loud. The same goes to you, hun." Oswald got up, looking as if he just woke up from a long nap. "Instant noodles sounds good to you, guys? Yes? Good. I'm not in the mood to cook anything else besides boiling water."

He dragged himself out of bed and waited for his own noodles. Still dealing with the outcome of his threesome, he managed to reach the door frame, where he held firmly. With a charming expression, he looked back at Daryl.

"You're not bound to anyone, tiger. But you can choose with whom you wanna make a bond. That's the thing with love."

Inadvertently, he held Terrence's hand. His grip made him feel the same as if he was holding Oswald's. But when he turned to his left and found the cheeky smile the crocodile was giving him, Daryl knew he wasn't Oswald. And he didn't feel the same thing he felt for Oswald.

And that was okay. Because Terrence deserved his own feeling. And he was eager to find it.

"You know, I can get used to that smile."

The crocodile moved forward, wanting that kiss previously denied. "Me too."

The Three Deaths and Lives of

Dmitri Ilyich Glaskov

Anhedral

The second time Dmitri died was at precisely 10:26 on the morning of 26 March 2039, out amid the parched scrub and malaria of the Yemeni *Tihāmah* and surrounded by his company.

Afterwards, he remembered that the sun's touch had been hot upon his jet-black winter fur. So very hot. Mid twenty-first century it might be, but even in this supposedly advanced age the world still hadn't found anything better than a werewolf's senses—scent and sight, touch and hearing—when it came to clearing mines. Which was all fine and well, but... Yemen, in late March? For northern wolves like him, it was a cruelty.

He remembered the tickle of sweat tracing down his paw. Was that why his fingerpads slipped onto the detonator? Or was it the distraction of Captain Holly's russet tail, flagging in the corner of his vision? The twin sister of the battalion commander had been not twenty yards ahead of him, down on her paws and knees, her shapely rear up in the air as she worked on her own landmine. She'd never been able to keep that tail of hers still while she worked.

Oh, why kid himself? He could put it down to Holly's rear, for sure.

The first time Dmitri died was at sunup one cold and baleful

April morning in Volgograd, just a few weeks shy of his nineteenth birthday. The year was 2037—in other words, sixteen years after the SAL epidemic first rampaged around the world.

He thought he had escaped it, that he was one of the lucky ones. He couldn't know for sure, of course; he'd never had the gene-test for Spontaneous Adolescent Lycanthropy. It was likely that his parents could not afford it. But it was equally possible that they simply refused to believe any offspring of theirs could take the fur, become one of the abominations so decried and shunned by church and state. Dmitri, therefore, had had no choice but to take his chance on that particular roulette-wheel of fate, to trust and hope that it was not his name on one of the five percent of slots that would give him the wolfish muzzle, the fangs and claws, the shedding problem every spring.

Dmitri shuddered awake that morning from a dream of animal intensity so visceral and clear he couldn't be quite certain if he was conscious or still in reverie.

The rich tang of the pines, the sharp and sudden sting of needles under paws. A raw and earthy musk clinging heavy in the air, the tickle of his muzzle buried deep within a ruff. His cock lodged fully in his mate, and oh how he wanted to thrust and thrust, but he was held immobile by a clasping heat. It didn't matter; the other male was doing all the work with his talented muscles down there, somehow squeezing at his thickness and his length over and again till he was mewling like a pup. But that was quite all right, because his mate was mewling too. Their little whines and cries merged as surely as their bodies, their voices twining one around the other before dissolving in the vastness of the night.

He felt his climax racing up, and his mate wasn't far off either. At the last moment she braces paws, arches her back, and cranes her lovely neck towards him. "Aaah!", she barks out. "YES!" Her gorgeous lime-green eyes flash wild beneath the moon. "I—I really cannot waaaait to have our p—pups!"

Wait... WHAT?

Dmitri felt a prickling of whiskers against cotton that was suddenly too rough, and a raging hardon sliding slick between his belly and the sodden sheets. He barely had time to register the new sensitivity of his shaft before the first swift sparks raced outwards from his groin to detonate somewhere deep and primal in his hindbrain. His cock swelled fuller still and jetted three times, four and five; he yelped at each release, whole body wracked with spasms. It was undoubtedly the most intense orgasm of his young life.

Gasping and panting in the aftermath, Dmitri rolled to his back, threw back the sheets, and put up a trembling paw to trace the unmistakable lines of a long and lupine muzzle.

"Oh, *yebat!*"

Maria met him for coffee the next morning. Well, she at least was having coffee; he could not, since he was currently Masked. The contraption tugged at the short fur of his muzzle and the longer guard-hairs of his muscled neck, and it was unpleasant to breathe through the thick gauze of the filters. Did the mask really prevent him from infecting humans, as the government had claimed? The question was academic: by law, he had to wear the thing whenever humans were nearby.

Maria, given the circumstances, seemed to be holding herself together pretty well.

"I'm sorry, Dmitri. It—it would never work. You must see that."

The newly-minted werewolf stared back at his childhood sweetheart as she reeled out a long list of all the reasons why the two of them could no longer marry. The church edicts that forbade it, for one thing; the stigma that would fall upon both families. And did he really want to wear that damned mask whenever he was within six feet of her?

It sounded like a very well-prepared speech. How long had she had it written up, he wondered? He'd never given any thought as to how he'd handle things if their situations were reversed; Maria, on the other hand, had clearly planned ahead.

Signally, the one thing she didn't mention was the matter of her own preference, the shifting sands of her affections. She probably thought she'd be doing him a kindness by this omission. But if she'd been trying to spare his feelings, it didn't work. He'd heard all he needed right at the start of her monologue, one momentary slip she hadn't even noticed. One word.

Dmitri, not Dima. She'd called him Dmitri.

He hadn't been Dmitri to her for a good long time. Not since the night of their first sweet stolen kiss. Three years ago it had been, but he could still recall that first quick, electric touch of her lips on his as if it were only yesterday.

Dima was lost to her now. Never again would she use that fond diminutive—well, not for him, at least.

He felt his ears go flat, felt his tail sag. If Maria saw him do it, she gave no sign. Dmitri did his best with pleasantries for a while, though all he could feel for those unending minutes was a leaden weight sinking ever deeper in his core. Eventually he made his excuses, and they parted.

He'd completed his mandatory wolf registration, he'd said the last of his goodbyes; the paperwork and the adieus, taken together, had occupied but a handful of days. Now, Dmitri sat panting and alone in the wolf-segregated carriage of the train that would carry him away from his old life and to the start of his new one in Murmansk Lycanthrope Commune. A small duffle-bag lay at his feet; his family would send along a few select belongings and keepsakes later.

His thick black pelt was taking a bit of getting used to. Dmitri panted, despite wearing only the thinnest of tank-tops and a pair of threadbare shorts. But then he noticed that the carriage's windows hinged open at the top, and soon he had the blissfully chill air of the Russian taiga washing in upon his unmasked face. He let his long tongue hang out. One positive aspect of moving to the Commune, he reflected, was that the wolves who lived there weren't obliged to wear anything other than their own fur.

Dmitri could hardly wait. He leaned back, let his golden eyes lid shut, and focused on the breeze upon his face and the thud and rumble of the carriage over ancient sleepers. All emotion drained from him, and it was only then that he perceived a single glimmer of brightness amid the overwhelming darkness of his fate. It had been there all week, but he hadn't been ready to see it until now.

He'd miss his family, yes he would. His friends; Maria too, despite how deeply her abrupt rejection had cut him. But this way, none of them would ever have to find out the truth he'd carefully kept hidden from all the world, ever since he admitted it to himself two long years before. He'd achieved this concealment by limiting his sociability, by making new friends only slowly.

There was a faint rustling in the carriage. Dmitri's ears flicked, and he opened his eyes; ah, just a newspaper left behind by the wolf who'd gotten off two stations before, the pages ruffling in the breeze. Dmitri reached idly across, and there, right there, on the random inner page that had been opened by the wind:

British Army Werewolf Veteran Decorated, Promoted
Reuters, London
3 May 2037
Captain Marcus Bolton, 33 Regiment Royal Engineers, today becomes the most highly-decorated werewolf to serve in the Scottish Armed Forces. Awarded the George Cross for conspicuous courage in extreme danger, Captain Bolton is a veteran of four mine-clearance tours of Afghanistan and two of Yemen. Three-time survivor of mine explosions, at 31 he is now promoted to Major and will lead the Lycanthrope Specialist Unit, which he helped to establish in 2036, in Aberdeenshire, Scotland. He will also work to expand his groundbreaking outreach programme, 'Wolves Against Landmines', in schools across the UK...

Dmitri blinked, and dropped the paper in his lap. Captain Bolton would never have been so lauded in Russia, where the advent of SAL had sparked an upswing of intolerance to the extent that werewolves were barely put up with at all. And the chances of a Russian werewolf like Dmitri fitting in? Dmitri knew *those* odds.

What was life like for wolves in newly-independent Scotland? He didn't rightly know. His only clue was that this Bolton fellow seemed to be crafting a werewolf-friendly army unit there.

One thing Dmitri did know for certain: he had a Scottish grandfather.

Dmitri Ilyich Glaskov applied for his Scottish passport two days after he arrived in Murmansk Commune, because by then he'd done his research. First, Bolton's new unit wasn't just werewolf-friendly, it was *all* werewolves; second, it was recruiting. And last—and this may have been the clincher—it promised a mask-free, clothing-optional environment.

A solid week of high pressure in December, and with it a constant seep of icy air from the Grampian hills and a lingering, heat-sapping mist that clogged the glens below. Humans grumbled and wrapped up warm, but Dmitri loved it. Werewolf climate; his kind of weather. It had put him in a good mood for days.

A mood that was about to be interrupted.

Captain Holly's voice echoed across the cavernous training room. "Dmitri? Ah, there you are! What's this, extra study again? Are you certain, wolf?"

"Ma'am!" The mine slipped from Dmitri's paws and fell to the bench with a dull thud. Cursing silently for being so easily flustered, he forced himself to take a big breath before yanking the blindfold from his eyes and coming to attention. "Just one more run through with these older models, ma'am. I flunked one of the tests, earlier today."

"Tsk." The russet wolf smiled back at him, shaking her head. Her breath fogged the chill air of the room as she padded up to him. "You silly wolf. You misidentified *one*, out of twenty; Dmitri, you're still top of your class. Wolf's gotta have some downtime too, y'know."

"Yes, ma'am," he replied promptly; he could hardly explain he'd been hoping for a perfect score, not without sounding conceited. "I'm, um, still not quite there with these older models..."

She paused at that. "Well, then," she sighed, flicking an ear at him and coming closer. "I'll help you with a handful, if it helps you finish sooner; the testing has to randomized anyway, to do it right. Blindfold on, cadet!"

The command was a blessing, if he was being honest with

himself, because this way he wouldn't run the risk of losing himself in the green flash of her eyes. He perked his ears to tie the knot loosely below them, and as he did he heard the thunk and scrape of the deactivated mines being rearranged on the scratched wood of the bench. A moment later Holly placed the first of her selection into his outstretched paws.

"You know the drill, Dmitri. This mine's been steam-cleaned inside and out, all trace of explosives gone—so for once, your nose won't help you to identify it. You gotta tell the model from touch alone."

He turned it round and round, fingerpads tracing the hard smooth cylinder, the projecting fuse on top. "OZM-4. Bounding mine, fragmentation type." He felt his muzzle twitch. "A nasty thing."

"Very good." *Clunk, thunk.* Now, this."

"Um..." A slightly smaller one this time, completely different shape. A thick disc perhaps three inches across, radial ribs. He counted off twelve of them with his thumb.

"TS-50. Um. Italian. Minimal metal, blast-resistant. Detonator's been removed. This here's a blanking plate."

"You got it. Last one for now, and then I really think we should call it a night."

Dmitri held out his paws as before, but the touch, when it came, was not of metal or hard plastic. Instead he got soft fur, a blunt claw nudging against his palm, the heat of fingerpads. He gasped, jolting backwards and nearly losing balance, but the female wolf caught him gently by his wrists.

"Dmitri."

He stood stock still and took a single shuddering breath. The cold air of the unheated room seemed to burn into his lungs.

One of her paws released, and he felt the tug of the blindfold as it loosened from his eyes. Green eyes flashed at him from a gentle face of lovely russet fur, and with that, the big black wolf was lost all over again.

"Wolves look out for wolves, Dmitri; sometimes, in this world, we're all we've got. Yes, Marcus and I are your commanding officers—but more importantly than that, we're werewolves, too."

She still held him by that single paw, although her touch was soft.

"And we're worried about you, young wolf."

"Ma—"

A frown and a single blink of green, bright as fresh spring grass, was all it took to silence him. "Nope. Not ma'am. Not now, not here tonight. Just another wolf. Just Holly."

Her fingerpads stroked his tenderly, just once, then finally released. She took a step, leant back against the bench all strewn with the hardware of human misery, folded her arms.

"Is everything all right, Dmitri? The other trainees missed you yesterday, y'know. That werewolf-only film night at the cinema in town—they wondered why you stayed back at the barracks. I know it isn't the first time you've kept your distance."

Dmitri felt his jaw crack open just a bit. He shut it again straight away with a snap. Holly was still smiling at him, her features soft, a quizzical wolf; her bright eyes flickered, rooting him right there.

"You are well liked here, Dmitri. Respected, too." She cocked her head. "I know it's rough for our kind back in your home country, but it was ballsy even so, leaving Russia like you did. If you ever wanted to talk that through, well, I've been told I'm a good listener. As it happens, Marcus is as well."

Dmitri shuffled his feet. "Ma—erm, H–Holly, I'd, um, really rather not talk about that. Not right now. If that's all right."

"Oh, you can relax, Dmitri." Ye gods, he thought, she could kill with just that smile. "I won't press you now, young wolf. Not now, not ever. But here's something to think about."

Her eyes narrowed, just a bit.

"Dangerous line of work we're in here, you and I. You knew that when you joined the Unit. It would be a shame not to enjoy what time we have, don't you think?"

"Umm..."

"You really don't see it, do you?" She gave him a sudden grin, a flash of wicked fang, and Dmitri blinked at the sudden change of tack. "Just take a look in the mirror sometime, Dmitri!

You're six-foot-six of athletic, black-morph Russian wolf in a world—well, in this Unit, anyway—of duns and greys and browns. You're charming, you're mysterious, you're aceing every class. You'll be an officer one day—"

"Oh, *ma'am!*"

She put up a paw to stop him. "In short, you could have any wolf you wanted in this camp. Instead of which, you're breaking hearts."

He couldn't find a single word with which to reply. Eventually, it was Holly who had to end the silence, gesturing him towards the exit as she did.

"That's it, Dmitri. I'm done, I've said my piece. After this, your private matters, outside your Army duties—they're your concern. I won't intrude, not as long as they don't affect your work; after all, we all have secrets of our own to keep." She blinked slowly, just the once, and gave an odd little crooked smile. Her tail was wagging as she walked, as if she were recalling some fond memory. "Believe it or not, young wolf, it's something that I understand all too well."

The third time Dmitri died was at sunrise on 5 July 2039.

That landmine back in Yemen had taken one of his eyes entirely and left him with cloudy, partial vision in the other. He was on the transplant waiting-list to get both of them replaced. And it wasn't just his eyes: his hearing and his sense of smell had also been drastically reduced. Overall, and somewhat ironically, he now functioned somewhere close to the level he'd been at before he became a wolf.

It was disorienting to be brought so low, so suddenly. Werewolf capabilities were very real; wolves didn't like to shout too loud about this, because most humans disliked lycanthropes quite enough already. But Dmitri missed his werewolf senses keenly. There were days when a black depressive mood would threaten to overwhelm him.

Oddly enough, the sensitivity of Dmitri's fur and skin to touch seemed only to have increased. He might drop a glass of water from the unexpected stab of cold in his paw. The slightest breeze upon his fur could make him quiver. The doctors, watching him in wonderment, had compared it to the enhancement of a blind man's hearing. Everything would settle down eventually, they'd said. He would be able to return to active duty.

It was that knowledge that kept him going through all of the pain and the frustration. And finally, on 4 July, he was ready to leave hospital and continue his recuperation—a healing process that would take place at the officer's quarters of his old training facility in Scotland, no less.

The home of Holly and of Marcus Bolton, both of whom had taken special leave to tend him.

"What's your preference, Dmitri?" Holly's voice issued, disembodied, from the kitchen's big walk-in refrigerator. "I can offer venison, or there's some lamb, fresh in today. Or, let's see..." A sound of rummaging, the slap of uncooked flesh on flesh. "Rabbits, hares. Take your pick."

Dmitri, sat fidgeting at the dining-table and unused to such an embarrassment of riches, managed to squawk out his reply. "R-Rabbit would be great, thank you."

Werewolves didn't stand on ceremony, not when it came to food. There was neither crockery nor cutlery, and the table's simple wooden top was varnished and wipe-clean. After that, fangs and raw flesh were the only items required. Conversation took a back seat as Holly and Marcus shared a haunch of venison, mock-fighting for the choicest bits, rending the dark flesh. Dmitri was more restrained at first, but soon decided it would be rude not to join in. Soon enough, the only sounds were those of tearing meat and crunching bones.

The resultant spectacle was just one of the reasons why human patrons at werewolf-frequented eateries tended to be few and far between.

Afterwards, sated, they took turns cleaning themselves up before lounging out in front of the big log fire. Dmitri was finally starting to relax; he glanced across at his male host, who was gnawing idly on a leg-bone much as a Victorian gentleman might have enjoyed a lazy cigar or whisky following his repast. The big gruff wolf in his pelt of rich grey-brown was horribly beaten up, his body scarred and one ear ragged; he looked a lot older than his thirty-three years. But the golden amber of his eyes was every bit as bright as Holly's green. His sister lay dozing close beside him, splayed out wantonly full length, belly to the fire.

Dmitri waited as patiently as he could for the other male to finish with his bone.

"Sir, ma'am, I—I wanted to thank you, both of you, for taking me in like this." His fur prickled, and his words seemed to clog within in his throat, but the question still demanded to be asked. "The hospital in Aberdeen... it had a recuperation ward, y'know..."

He trailed off then, coming close to muttering an oath. Was he wolf, or mouse? But his words seemed to have sufficed. Marcus and Holly tilted their heads towards one another, ears flicking, and seemed to take a breath as one.

"We know, Dmitri." It was Holly, and her tone was hollow, a thing he'd never heard before. "But we owe at least this much to you, for failing in our duty of care towards you."

He felt his ears go flat. He didn't understand. "Duty of care?"

The lithe female moved into a cross-legged squat, an odd, uncomfortable-looking pose for her. She did seem strangely unsettled, but he couldn't trust enough to his crappy vision to be sure. "That's right. Do you remember the blindfold test we did together, just you and I?"

How could he forget that night? "I remember."

"I said then that I would only ask about your personal life if it was affecting your work." Her shoulders sagged, and her tail hung limp and still behind her. "But even when I knew for certain that it was, I didn't act—and that's probably what got you hurt. You're not very good at hiding your emotions, Dmitri. I hope you never change that."

The very air in the room seemed to thicken about him. The pops and crackles of the fire were suddenly too loud, even to his banged-up ears. "Hiding... emotions?"

Holly was getting to her feet, padding towards him. He gulped, startling back, but then she fixed him with those grass-green eyes, and of course at that point it was far too late. Holly drew him, quite unresisting, into a gentle embrace. His fur seemed to be on fire everywhere she touched.

"Do not be concerned, Dima. Honestly, I'm flattered."

He gasped. *What* had she just called him?

"As is her mate." Marcus was approaching then as well. He winked at Dmitri. Actually *winked.* "Because you weren't just looking at Holly here, now were you?"

Oh, gods. They were mates. Not just siblings then, oh no. And they'd both seen him looking at, at...

Dmitri's legs, army-trained as they were, seemed ready to collapse beneath him. He was dead, he was a dead wolf. They were going to tear him apart right there and then and hang him up in that damned cold-store till they were hungry once again. *That's* why he was in their home.

He shut his eyes.

And so it was that, when the big male wolf kissed him fully on the muzzle, Dmitri was even less prepared than he might otherwise have been.

...sometimes, in this world, we're all we've got...

...you could have any wolf you wanted in this camp...

Any wolf. *Oh.*

Any. Wolf.

It was as if there was a hotline between his muzzle and his sheath. His eyes snapped open wide. "Mmmpfff....!"

Marcus pulled back then, but not by much. He was grinning, his long wolf tongue lolling purple from his jaws. The older werewolf cocked his head.

"Sometimes a wolf's just got to go for it. You're lucky I held back with my tongue."

Holly slapped him gently across his muzzle, battle-scarred as it was.

"You *dog.*"

But Marcus, still smiling, was already sinking to his knees. Holly sighed, then whispered to Dmitri, gentler, as she stroked between his ears:

"Go ahead, Dima. Just try and save a bit for me."

Dmitri drifted into wakefulness and stared up at the ceiling. Dawn's sunlight bathed his fur, but it was a lazy, pleasant heat—not like Yemen, no, not like that at all.

His body came alive to sparks of touch. A revelation: three wolves to a bed works just fine. A big male wolf was nuzzled at his shoulder; on his other side, a gorgeous russet female curled tight against his hip. She'd fallen asleep with a paw over one of his, held close to her lean belly; her fur there was the colour of autumn leaves. Dmitri's fingerpads found a crusty patch—himself, or Marcus?—and he found himself hoping that the officers' quarters had a big shower.

Memories flooded back, coalescing from an erotic haze, becoming more coherent. The wrap of his tongue around the sex of another male at last; so swollen it had been, the flesh so warm and sensuous, the nudge of it into his muzzle so utterly, completely *right*. Him knot-deep inside Holly, the flash of her glorious green eyes down at him, her pupils widening as he flooded her with warmth.

Dmitri sighed out a deep breath, wonderfully contented. No more secrets, no, not now. Finally, he was whole. Finally, he'd come home.

And thus it was, with this epiphany, that the third life of Dmitri Ilyich Glaskov came to an end. How should he go about living his fourth? The black wolf, listening to his mates to either side breathing in and out with easy synchrony, pondered it. His fourth life, he realised, would be his alone to shape.

Ambrosia and Nectar

Nathan Hopp

I feared Erastos and Alcaeus would not come that day.

Mount Olympus towered over the hilly landscape as I waited at its base. A lone owl hooted in the distance alongside a lonely songbird, signaling that evening would arrive soon if one was blind to the descending sunset to the west. Or the cool spring wind blowing in one's cheekfur, combined with the gentle warmth of Helios' burning grin in the sky.

"Where are you? How long must I torture myself by standing here?"

I wondered if this was what Hades felt when he first waited for his beloved Queen to fly in his arms that first winter. Had he worried that Demeter would not abide by their agreement, and separate her offspring from his husband once more? The next time he joined another symposium on Olympus, I hoped Hades would give me some further insight, if Alcaeus and Erastos did not…did not….

"No," I scolded myself. "You foolish wolf. They will come."

I tried my best to focus on the tales me and my sister Artemis were told as cubs, such as how the ancient base of this very mountain was one of many battlefields during the Titanomachy. Unfortunately, no matter how hard I recounted such memories, my mind returned to the thoughts of a certain red deer and black-maned lion.

Speaking of whom, I perked my ears at an unnatural sound and glanced down the stone path. At first, I considered it a trick of the sunlight, or a mirage of my hopeful imagination, yet the sight of two figures hiking up to the base of the mountain did not cease.

They both wore simple wool tunics, with the larger male—a muscular gold-furred lion with a black mane—gripping a walking stick and the smaller male—a tall red stag who seemed younger, despite being the same age as his counterpart—in a silky chlamys that draped around his lithe frame. Both of them walked closely beside each other in comfortable tandem, though I could tell from this distance how many times the deer secretly marveled at the rear end of his travelling companion.

I chuckled, both in amusement and in weightless relief. Typical Erastos.

From the first days of manhood to today, he and Alcaeus had grown steadily into masculine young furs. I immediately thought back to the day I first laid my eyes on them, two strapping boys not a week past their eighteenth summer, sneaking out from their respective homes at twilight to enjoy themselves in private exploration. They both lived in the mortal city-state of Dion, near the base of Mount Olympus, with the deer born the son of a war general and the lion the son of a talented poet and part-time athlete.

One of them would later speak of meeting by chance when Alcaeus' father hired Erastos and his family to furnish his office. This occurred years ago in their youth, and both fell in love at first sight. They were also aware of the consequences of what would happen if word escaped to the public that the son of a war general willingly submitted himself to another man of lower class. Yet that night, under cover of darkness once I rode my chariot away, I watched them make love for the first time across countless future nights.

And each time I watched from afar, I never came harder in my eternal life. Or stifled any euphoric moans and shudders with such previous strength.

Now at long last, after twelve months apart, all three of us saw each other across the great length of the stone path. Without a single word or moment of hesitation, I hurried down the pathway towards them. Neither bothered to wait either, lunging into my arms. Erastos needed to lean up to fully embrace me, while Alcaeus owned little trouble, given his immense stature and soft demeanor.

"I have missed you both so much."

Erastos whimpered into my shoulder. "As have I, Apollo," he softly murmured.

"Me too…." Alcaeus nuzzled into my warm neck.

Silently, we held each other until I broke this tranquil memory by lifting both of their muzzles to meet mine. My lips melted into Alcaeus' first, tasting his feline tongue against mine before I parted and kissed Erastos next. He eagerly leaned up to welcome me, his tongue lapping at my lips as a giggle emitted from mine. Yet soon, a moan escaped from the back of my throat when I heard deep purring behind me, and Alcaeus' cold nose pressing into the side of my neck.

"Hehe, that tickles," I playfully swatted the large feline. "You know I'm—ah!"

"Heh, I know."

"We must depart at once though." I had to pull away slightly, amused by the deer and lion's reluctance to let me go. "The hour is approaching, and I want to make tonight more memorable than any other."

"But, Apollo…." Erastos spoke up, clasping my paw and offering an uneasy smile. "What of…you know…our answers?"

The air grew thicker. Even Alcaeus, standing behind me as a silent statue, became quiet to hear my response.

"There is plenty of time, beloveds. For now,"—I smiled softly and glanced between them, ignoring the faint pain in my chest—"I simply wish to be with you both and enjoy our time together."

Erastos whimpered.

"Do not worry," I soothed him. "You and Alcaeus can give me your answers later tonight when we have…reacquainted ourselves. Hehe."

Sudden smirks crossed their muzzles, Erastos' more so.

"Now then." I clapped my paws thrice.

Across the horizon, a bright light emerged from the distance, descending closer until it came into view. My beloveds both held their paws to their eyes, shielding themselves from the intense illumination of my chariot, led by three beautiful steeds made of molten sunlight.

"Ugh," Erastos groaned, "can you please dim it down again?"

"Yeah," Alcaeus agreed. "We wonder how you tolerate this brightness!"

I could not help but laugh softly. "You mortals and your sensitive eyesight…." A quick snap of my fingers, and it dimmed down to a bearable glow, allowing them to fully see. "I must help guide Helios in his descent, but I believe we can arrive to our destination atop the mountain once my task is complete?"

"Our…destination?" Alcaeus questioned me, his eyes widening with the same wonder from when I first revealed myself. "You mean…we are going…."

Erastos finished for him, "Are we finally going…up to…the top?"

My tail wagged vigorously behind me. "We are!"

"W-Will we be seeing the other gods?" my deer stammered out, his ears perked with intense curiosity. "W-Will Z—I mean…will every other god be there?"

Most mortals remained cautious to utter the names of a god in their presence, even in that of another god's. Doing so gave someone like me power over them. Both he and Alcaeus, when we first knew each other, preferred to call me by "Lord" or "Sire," much to my embarrassment. This did not change until months later, when the lion said, "I love you, Apollo," by accident. Nowadays, they never wavered to casually say my name but remained cautious when speaking of the other gods.

"Hopefully not to the point they will brawl again." I laughed again, stepping into my chariot and offering a paw to each of them. "Now, we cannot delay too long…."

Though hesitant at first, our beloved lion eventually took my paw when Erastos and I guided him behind the chariot's golden railing, his muscular side and pectorals sandwiching me between him and our beloved deer. He pressed his body into mine, the boy's antlers thankfully shortened so my eye would not be poked out, and I could not ignore their bulges and perked buttocks against my thighs any longer. I could feel myself pant with delight, these two handsome males wrapping an arm around me with a single paw grasping the front of the chariot.

Yet duty called to me.

My paws grabbed onto the reins. "Hya!"

As fast as doves in morning light, we soared far above the clouds and into the heavens. Both of my beloveds yelped with fright at first, tightening their grips onto me as I laughed against the howling winds. However, they eventually opened their eyes to the wondrous sight beneath us: the mortal realm in all its glory from above.

As my steeds led this chariot across the sky, Alcaeus and I marveled at the view of the land and sea. The lion could not resist looking downward, nearly losing his foothold in the chariot. My comforting paw eased him, and I could feel a purr resonate from the back of his throat, down his strong arm and into my stroking fingers while I guided my chariot.

As I commanded Helios' descent over the horizon, Erastos amused me when he slowly reached out of the chariot, his paws feeling the clouds passing us by. His fingers sliced through each one, happiness bubbling from his lips when water dripped down his paws and a huff of cloud escaped his grasp. I entertained him further by soaking us in some clouds. Alcaeus—his fur and chlamys dampened along with ours—wasn't pleased by this, but Erastos' laughter and mine pulled the lion into our joined merriment.

Yet seeing the youthful stag and his smile only returned me to what I saw that night just the night before. And the emotions I felt watching from afar as he cried in bed, having argued earlier with his father.

"Father, I am not lying to you! Apollo has made me his beloved mate!"

"Son, you will quit these fantasies, or so help me, by the gods, I will strike you!"

"It is no fantasy, Father! Alcaeus and I are beloveds to Apollo! He has

asked that we—"

SMACK!

"Foolish cub! You are my son and are destined to be my successor!"

"Apollo?" Alcaeus called me. "Is it finished?"

I blinked back to this reality, finding Helios finally finished his descent. The stars above could be visibly seen, from the mighty belt of Orion to Perseus immortalized by his heroic deeds.

"Are you well, love?" Erastos spoke up, concern glinting in his beautiful green orbs. "Is there something on your mind?"

"Y-Yes, my beloveds," I replied with a wag of my tail, tickling the backs of their legs. "I am fine. Let us depart to Olympus, shall we? Hya!"

My chariot danced from the stars down to Earth. Peeking through the clouds and shining just as brilliantly as any rainbow stood the crystalline palaces on the summit.

I gently landed the chariot at the courtyard entrance. One of Hephaestus' crafted servants graciously took the reins to guide my steeds into the stables (both my beloveds couldn't resist staring at the chromium and marble automatons), while another held open the gates for us. I did not even have to tell them Erastos and Alcaeus—mortal as can be—were guests and allowed admission. The deer and lion's awe did not cease however when we delved deeper into the grand hall. Statues of every mineral on Earth lined the corridor alongside some lit torches, while a brilliant skylight trailed down to the inner open courtyard leading to the other palaces.

"It is beautiful, Apollo," Erastos breathed at last. "Do you live here?"

"Heh, of course he lives here, Erastos!" Our beloved lion stifled his snickering to ask, "I think he meant if you live in this particular building?"

"I do not," I shook my muzzle, tousling the small cervine's headfur. This annoyed him slightly, much to me and Alcaeus' amusement. "No, each dweller on Olympus is given a palace of theirs to rule."

When we entered the inner courtyard, surrounded by a

patterned marble floor, torches and blooming roses no doubt planted by Aphrodite, Erastos pointed to the largest castle of all.

"I assume that one is your father's?" he guessed correctly.

My smirk resumed. "He loves to show his extravagance."

In all honesty, I would have gone further to say Zeus had the Cyclops build his palace merely to compensate for his…inadequacies. Saying such things aloud would have resulted in one's instant demise, especially if spoken on Olympus, let alone to his face.

"Hello, Son!"

I whirled to my left to find a familiar bearded wolf wearing the finest of white robes, his hairy chest comfortably exposed, and the eagle wings on his back draped back. Statues in the mortal world did not depict him as having the latter, but eagles were seen nevertheless as being one of his many symbols besides a bolt of lightning.

Both Alcaeus and Erastos breathed in amazement. "Y-You are…" the latter started to say.

I bowed in respect. "Good evening, Father. I have completed my daily task."

"Obviously," he chuckled mightily. When his eyes fell onto the two mortals standing nervously beside me, the lion and deer bowed their heads. "Oh, that is not so necessary, lads! You are guests in my domain after all!"

"A-Apologies, my Lord," Erastos muttered in fear and immense respect.

Meanwhile, Alcaeus wrapped his rope-like tail around mine, very protectively.

"We are honored to be here, my Lord," he greeted Zeus with bravery in his voice. "Your son has given us a tour of Mount Olympus, and thus far, it is a spectacular sight to behold."

A cocky grin etched itself onto the old wolf's muzzle. "Thank you, lad. And what are your names?"

My deer stepped forward first, placing a paw on his chest. "I am Erastos of Dion, son of General Olysseus."

My lion then introduced himself next. "I am Alcaeus, also of Dion, my Lord. Son of the Dionese poet Alexios."

"Hmm." My father glanced between them, then down to me. "I can see why you would fancy them both. They are handsome and cute. I trust you want some privacy while indulging in your carnal desires tonight, Apollo?"

Both my beloveds blushed fiercely beneath their cheekfur, the lion visibly curling his tail and the stag trying to make himself smaller on the spot. Before I could even be given the chance to discreetly roll my eyes, Zeus patted my shoulder.

"May I have a word with you alone first?"

I normally would have objected, but the expression on his face was adamant, and his eyes gazing to them—knowingly curious—reminded me that he knew too of the Oracle's prophecy.

"You may." I smiled assuredly back to my beloveds. "I must speak to Zeus about something important, but it will not be for long. You both make yourselves comfortable in my palace in the meantime, okay?"

"O-Okay." Erastos nodded sheepishly.

I kissed him, then Alcaeus who, though uncertain at first, simply nodded.

"Okay, Apollo," he murmured.

A grin spread across my coy muzzle.

"Good kitten." He blushed and embarrassedly growled. "Heh."

I ordered one of the chromium servants nearby, a naked leopardess probably inspired by Aphrodite, to escort my beloveds as I followed Zeus into his palace. Like any other built on Mount Olympus, the walls were composed of the finest of crystals and gold. The statues inside, the largest of which depicted Hera and him during the happier days of their marriage, lined the way up to a marvelous throne carved into the walls. And Zeus gladly sat atop it to stare down at me.

"Apollo," he asked, "have they given you an answer yet? Do they desire to ascend to godhood?"

My mind drifted. It had been almost five years since I first introduced myself to Erastos and Alcaeus, two of the brightest and most wonderful of mortals I ever formed a relationship with.

Unlike my other conquests of love, not only had it lasted the longest (Hyacinthus only second) without much conflict or drama, but the feelings I held toward them each grew into passionate fires in my chest. And they would not cease, burning even brighter when a wondrous thought crossed my mind.

"Not yet, Father."

"It has been an entire year since you've last seen either of those mortals, Apollo." He sighed. "Those Oracles in your temple at Delphi said that if you gave them both a year by themselves, to contemplate if godhood was worth abandoning their mortality to be with you, then they would be by your side forever."

"I am fully aware, Father." My tail twitched as I stared down to the marble floor. "I just…fear if it means something else entirely. If one of us does not want to be together, then neither of us will. We agreed to that at least…."

"I could always speak to them alone if that is so," he suggested.

My eyes glared daggers at him. "Do not even think of harming my beloveds, Zeus."

"By Cronos, I would never do such a thing!" He cackled heartily, standing to his feet and descending to my level. "Surely, you would know better of me."

He reexamined my expression for a moment, then sighed once more. I sensed sincerity in his next lecture to me, something rarely witnessed.

"In all honesty, Apollo…I am fully aware that I'm the last god to speak to when it comes to true love. In truth, if I may be so frank, there is no Olympian on this mountain who is perfectly content in the relationships we've formed with mortals."

"What of Eros and Psyche?" I pondered aloud. "She was mortal once."

"You are correct." He nodded. "But the god of love and sex has never cared for and prized two beloveds at once, has he? No god has. What you possess with Erastos and Alcaeus is beautiful and equal, but…do you love them both, as much as they love each other?"

The most complete understatement of the current eon. Before I was able to retort his statement, however, doubt crept in when I remembered the prior night. It placed an emptying depression in my chest, which grew larger the further I remembered how devoted Erastos was to his father. How he trained hard with the soldiers yet was saddened that the elder stag didn't allow his son to venture into any battle, and how victories in sparring were never enough.

"I must return to them now." I pulled my robes closer, still damp with water.

Zeus flapped his wings. "Good luck to you, Son."

The Palace of Apollo shined near the eastern side of the summit. Like the others, it was carved from marble and polished from crystals. A pavilion entrance led down a corridor to my main andron, displaying a statue of me between two short hallways. The right one led to the spacious bedroom where I had taken some mortals as lovers (tonight, hopefully two more…permanently), while the left led to where I found them in the balcony garden.

As a gift from Helios, I could keep a sliver of sunlight for my possession, keeping it as a decorative centerpiece on the pavilion. Compared to the rest of Mount Olympus bathed in torchlight, my balcony glowed like a miniature sun hovering above.

Any other mortal would have been overwhelmed by such a sight, but not Erastos or Alcaeus. I had missed their awe, as they had already stripped off their clothes and hung them to dry on the branch of a laurel tree nearby. This left the mortals completely naked as they playfully wrestled on a patch of grass. I was momentarily distracted by Alcaeus' feline butt as it bounced behind him before finally speaking up.

"Hello, beloveds."

Both froze in their stances, gripping the other's arms. My deer looked over our lion's shoulder to me, lowering his heated ears and growing an impressive erection.

"We-We were just waiting for you," Alcaeus stammered shyly, distracting me once more at the way his half-erect sexuality swung in the air. The musk alone sent me back to when I first tasted his precum.

"Heh, do continue, will you?" I offered, sitting down to watch. "I enjoy this view more than the other one beside us."

"A-Actually," the lion continued, "A-Apollo…I…"

"May I watch you two, please?" Erastos asked for him. The deer stood beside our lion and, patting the shy feline's rear, licked his lips without tearing his eyes away from mine. "Alcaeus has talked much of how he missed sporting with you, Apollo. I have also missed your rivalry for dominance."

Mutual smirks suddenly etched across our muzzles, Alcaeus and I.

I stood back to my footpaws and promptly shed my clothes and trinkets. Erastos stepped aside and leaned back on the warm grass. Meanwhile, Alcaeus stretched his muscled arms as I merely waited for him to be ready.

"Today might be the day I finally beat you, Apollo," he chuckled. "Try not to cry like a girl when I beat you."

I played along with his boastful words. "You may try, but my Oracles have told me by tonight, I'll be having you purr like a little kitten…."

Alcaeus growled and lunged for my legs first. I instinctively wrapped my arms over his back to stop him from making me fall, but the lion became persistent. He gripped my lower buttocks and tried to fight dirty by tickling my hole, and I managed to let out a low moan before using my strength to toss him over my shoulders. Our backs impacted against the dirt, making us gasp for air, yet Alcaeus was quick enough to shift back up and lock his arms around my torso.

"Do you yield, pup?" he teased.

"Not yet…" I giggled between gritted teeth. "Not yet, little kitten!"

My elbow struck him in the abdomen, and I reversed our positions. Now my hardened cock grazed his backside as I gripped paws around his torso, pushing him against the grass. Alcaeus gulped beneath me, especially from the way my phallus curved along his crack. I nearly expected him to yield when my focus drew to the deer watching us nearby.

Erastos intently watched without pulling his paw away from his erection. Blushing and panting, the deer stroked his slick length up and down, slow, steady, and fast as Alcaeus and I continued to wrestle. Normally, I would have looked away had Erastos not flashed a hazy smile, pumping his shaft amid a high theatrical moan. It certainly made me leak further.

Alcaeus flashed his fangs. "Thank you, love!"

He used the opportunity to fall backwards, this time pinning me down with my back against the dirt. The lion did not wait to shift his body and lock my wrists above my wolfish ears, his erection now slickening my stomach with his precum. I tried not to moan too much at feeling his balls touch my sheath.

"That was dirty of you, Erastos!" I groaned.

"I am not sorry, Apollo!"

How could he be ashamed, masturbating at the sight of two powerful men pinning each other down for dominance?

Our Erastos and I connected through our interests in the arts and some history. The young stag's fondness for archery always heralded days spent practicing in the woods. Of course, he could never compete with my bow and arrow's divine accuracy, but when I gifted him a finely crafted bow I commissioned from Athena, the lad's precision with an arrow rivaled that of mine.

Meanwhile, Alcaeus and I connected through our interests in sports such as this. Especially without any strip of cloth to obstruct our physical limits. In spite of being a head taller than I, the lion's large body did not crush me. It could not crush me, but I still tried my best not to use all my strength or stamina to end the match quickly. I wanted to make this last as much as possible. I also wanted to prolong Erastos' climax for tonight.

An hour into the match, the lion had yielded twice while I did once. Our furry bodies had grown damp from sweat, to the point our tails wagged like weighed paddles. Even strong Alcaeus had begun to complain about his sore legs yet did not surrender.

Could not, more likely.

"How has the past year been for you, Alcaeus?"

We began circling each other once more, our arms outstretched and ready for any offensive.

"Busy," he answered, staring between me and our deer (I would not be distracted again!). "It is surprising how much time one must devote to athletics and poetry. Father is very interested in having me follow in his works…."

I curiously grinned. "And what of you, Erastos? Have you and Alcaeus been having fun while we've been away?"

"It has been challenging without you," he exhaled breathily behind me, "but we have endured…."

"By the way," Alcaeus interrupted upon some realization, "my father is aware of my relationship with you!"

That certainly gained more of my undivided attention.

"And he believes you?" I raised an eyebrow towards the feline. "He believes his son is the beloved of an Olympian god?"

"So long as I bring you back and allow Mother to cook dinner after tonight." He laughed. "He would want me to prove your existence, but he will be even more impressed when I finally win more matches—"

I did not give him time to finish that lone statement. Seconds later, I made the lion lose his footing and held him once more on the ground, his arms held in a vice as I ground my peeking sheath into his backside. All as I heard Erastos' breathing and mindful strokes nearby.

"Mmm, do you yield again, Alcaeus?"

"N-No…" he answered, so I replied by nibbling his round, heated ear, inflaming our aching desires. "Ahhh! Y-Yes, I yield!"

I released his arms and helped the large mortal to his footpaws, then teased his member prior to sniffing the air.

"Dinner is coming, beloveds," I announced. "To the dining room."

"Wonderful!" Alcaeus healed quickly from his beaten pride, wrapping am arm around my torso, "Come on, Erastos! I believe I smell roasted boar!"

"Please let me release myself, Apollo," he whined, his member stiffly throbbing when he walked beside us.

"Control yourself, love," I whispered hungrily into his ear. "Let us wait until after dinner before we cum too. Hehe."

That only made the youthful deer's cock even harder, much

to our yearning entertainment. Erastos though, not as much.

True to the mortal legends, gods did not consume regular food. Instead we dined on heavenly ambrosia bread and nectar thick enough to rival honey. A single drop of the latter could wash away any defilement of an ethereal being, while a mixture of both would retain any immortality. However, I did employ some of Olympus' chromium servants to cook mortal foods for my starving beloveds.

"Ahhh, fassolatha…with sardines," Alcaeus' maw watered as we sat down together. "You remembered my favorite!"

"And mine…." Erastos practically drooled over the bits of meat mixed into his fassolatha and salad. Around the table, the chromium servants also baked some gastrins and loukoumades dipped in honey, which I assumed to be tasty as well. "By the gods, they smell so delicious…."

"Dine then." I laughed. "Nothing is stopping either of you."

As my lion and stag devoured their foods, I had passed the time by playing my lyre. Neither of them complained, and in fact listened with unabated interest.

The song I played for them was titled "A Vague Hope for Grass," a hymn I dedicated to a nomadic family of fennecs who traveled all the way from Egypt for a better life. I witnessed when the father first stepped foot on the beaches of southern Crete, happy to have escaped the sweltering heat and the tyranny of the pharaohs. Their maiden daughter also gave me some…inspiration for writing a couple of erotic poems on the side.

Suddenly, my fingers on the lyre became mournful as I thought of her fate. She had been unaware of my watchful eyes, and when I revealed myself to her as a god foreign from her homeland, the fennec died of shock. Right before my very eyes.

My worry from earlier resurfaced into my music. The cheerful music transformed into a melancholy that made my paws tremble slightly. Would Alcaeus agree to join me on Mount Olympus? Would Erastos, in spite of his controlling father? Would I be once again be denied the chance to have my beloveds by the side?

Why did my beloveds always quickly leave me? Daphne, Bolina, Ocroe, Leucates…they all left me. Perhaps the Fates condemned me to live forever alone without any form of love—

"Apollo, why are you crying?"

I abruptly paused the performance, realizing too late that tears had welled up in the corners of my eyes. And both of my beloveds stared at me with immediate concern in theirs.

"Hmm?" Feigned ignorance never convinced either of them in the past, but I tried anyway, wiping my eyes dry as I set my lyre gently back on the table. "Some dust, my beloveds. Do not worry…."

Indeed, neither seemed content with my response, or composure. I was surprised to next open my eyes and find Alcaeus' arm wrapped around my torso and Erastos' around my stomach. In silence, I fell into their arms like a stone into a pond.

Giving a deep sigh, I knew the moment of truth had finally come.

"Can we…go to my bedroom?"

Neither snickered or grew hot from the suggestive comment, only nodding as I led them inside.

The sunlight faded into darkness we gladly welcomed, with bluish moonlight flooding over the mattress. Unlike mortal beds, mine came crafted from the bark of an ancient Mastika tree and was draped in silk gifted to me by a weaver from the East.

For now, all three of us did not admire the soft bedding or the aromatic smells rising from some lit candles. Hopefully, not yet.

"Why didn't you eat with us?" Erastos suddenly asked.

In truth, I did not want to drink the ambrosia and nectar and suddenly feel both digest inside my stomach as a reminder of their possible answer. I decided not to answer, and instead grasped one paw around both of theirs, positioning myself between the well-sculpted lion and our effeminately formed stag.

"It is because you're wondering about our answers, is that correct?" Alcaeus glanced between us.

I slowly nodded. "…yes."

"Well, then." Alcaeus spoke first, scooting closer to me as my heart raced in uncertain fear. "I have…no, *we* have decided…yes."

My crestfallen ears straightened upward.

"What did you…?"

"We said 'yes.'" Erastos leaned into my neck and hugged me tightly. "We want to become gods with you. We want to be immortal and spend the ends of eternity as your husbands…and you as ours."

Alcaeus said something first.

"Erastos and I thought it would be best to speak about our decision before trekking up Mount Olympus," he explained, "and through the turmoil spent apart these past twelve months, deep down…he and I know we cannot endure another moment from you. And you?"

"But…But what of your parents?" I pointed out, my mind racing alongside my immortal heart, which refused to slow down. "Your father, what will he think?"

"What he thinks and desires of me doesn't matter." The handsome buck stated. "It never mattered, not when I have the chance to live forever with the men I love."

"Will you not miss your families?" I questioned them further. "Will you not miss the simplest pleasures of mortality? I do not—"

"Apollo."

"—know if you realize how serious this is. You will live forever and—"

Alcaeus silenced me with a kiss, and Erastos a mighty hug.

"We did not travel all this way to let you go again," the buck sniffled into my fur.

No other words could ever be needed. The fearful barriers next gave way to the incoming floodwaters of Eros, unyielding sexual love.

Two pairs of paws roamed my sensitive sides, my own fingers exploring the well-sculpted abs and muscles hidden beneath a thick lion pelt. After pulling his lips from mine, Alcaeus raised his head to kiss Erastos behind me whilst I sniffed the musk of his pillowed mane. The three of us already could not get enough of each other sitting up, and instead fell backwards onto the silky bedsheets.

Alcaeus straddled my stomach, devouring my lips to distract me until Erastos suckled the responsive member from my sheath. When his tongue tasted my swollen knot, it drove me mad.

"Ahhh," I placed my paws to Alcaeus' sides, humping into the deer's velvety maw. "Ah, I have yearned for this day so much…."

"As have we," Alcaeus huskily answered.

Of course, Erastos replied by licking the tip of my manhood, eliciting another moan from me that melted back into our lion's lips. My cries grew even more prominent when Alcaeus' tongue slipped to lap at the nape of my sensitive neck, causing my tail to tickle our attentive deer's abdomen.

"S-Stop that, please." The red deer then coyly warned me, "I will not continue if you do not quit, Apollo."

I relented, though Alcaeus grew bold enough to nip at my neck like a feline would in tasting a slice of well-cooked boar. This made me gasp, especially when the lion's teeth nearly pierced my skin.

"Easy there, Alcaeus!" I gasped, twitching my ears in pleased delight. "I am no prized meat."

"You taste like prized meat though," he nibbled harder. "Then again, it sounds like Erastos is the one enjoying the prized meat between your legs."

We laughed, and it seemed he retorted by pushing his antlers into the lion's ass.

"Ow! Ow! Ow!" Alcaeus growled disparagingly down at Erastos. "Please do not do that again, Erastos…."

He briefly paused his sucking to say, "Your butt is as hard and firm as marble, Alcaeus."

He growled more.

"Fine, I will not do that again…." He returned to my aching length again.

"Typical stag," Alcaeus playfully grumbled.

I laughed again at this display of comradery, pulling Alcaeus back into a long kiss and bucking my hardened erection back and forth into Erastos' velvet lips. His tongue would loll out to coat the underside of my scrotum, driving me mad in a way that almost willed me into a forceful climax. However, it required every strength in me not to do so just yet.

At some point into the night, all three of us lay together on the bed, panting and trading tongues in a tripled kiss; my body acted as a link between them on either side of me, arms wrapped around their sweaty bodies while my fingers patted their relaxing muscles.

I had been sucking on Erastos' tongue, and him to mine, for some time when we both noticed Alcaeus sniffling. We turned our heads to find the lion, lustful just minutes ago, now tearfully wiping his eyes with his free wrist.

"I-I am sorry if I am giving him more affection, Alc—"

"No, it is not that…" he whined, more from embarrassment than sadness. "It is something else."

Looking back to Erastos once more, he and I sat back to our knees and each held a paw of the lion's. The lust from before immediately replaced itself with comforting interest.

My golden tail curled around him. "Is something on your mind, beloved?"

Alcaeus spoke, "It is nothing."

"Whatever you think or ponder about,"—Erastos squeezed his right paw—"it always matters to us."

"Indeed," I nodded. "Now…do not hide what you are feeling, Alcaeus. We will listen."

Neither of us judged the lion when his posture and brave demeanor began to fall.

"It is just…during our time apart, Apollo…,"—he hiccupped, then composed himself—"I was terrified you would realize you would become bored of us."

My heart nearly snapped in two like a twig upon hearing Alcaeus' words. Even Erastos seemed to shiver beside me and stare in incredible sympathy when the mortal deer heard what Alcaeus feared the most. He likely did not know about this either.

"I-I know now it is a silly thought," he said, trembling, "but I feared that would become the case for us. We are mortals…and you are a god. I feared you would one day come to regret taking us as eternal lovers on Olympus…."

In the space of several seconds, I let go of his paws, nodded to Erastos and helped him pull the foolish lion into a strong, circular hug.

"We both held silly thoughts," Erastos murmured into the furs of our necks, "but no longer…."

"Agreed," I looked up to peck Alcaeus' lips again. "I will never grow bored of either of you. If such a thought crossed my mind, I would have the three-headed hellhound Cerberus eat me alive first."

Alcaeus chuckled and wiped his nose. "You would not."

"I would." A sudden thought crossed my mind, and I whispered the same idea into Erastos' ear. A heartbeat later and the youthful lad smirked back in agreement. "Lay back then for us."

The dutiful deer lowered his back to the sheets and, raising his legs into the air, revealed the winking entrance beneath his teardrop tail. As he did this, I positioned myself behind him and levitated a small jar of olive oil to us. I grasped it in my paw and started lathering my fingers in it when I finally heard that deep purring behind me.

I craned my neck to find Alcaeus watching us, licking those chops of his. "Well?"

"What?" The lion tilted his muzzle in confusion.

A soft smile spread across my lips. As I gently stretched Erastos' ring with my slick fingers (earning us musical moans that got me and Alcaeus' cocks to twitch), my free paw handed him the jar.

Two seconds later, he understood.

"Y-You want me to—"

"Yes."

"But you are a god," he argued in spite of his manhood growing harder. "It is not—"

"Who is to say it is not right?" I countered the lion. My tail swished aside to give him access. "I am a god, but so will you be. So will Erastos. And besides, this has been a fantasy for him since we met."

Erastos could only voice his approval in moans, thanks to the movements of my fingers inside his moist walls. I probably touched his prostate more than once.

"P-Please," he begged in addiction to me, "make me yours, Apollo!"

I slyly caressed his chin and neck.

"As you wish." Then I dared Alcaeus, "Can you handle breeding an Olympian, kitten?"

That certainly made him bold. After lathering his paw and roughly stretching my virginity, assuring my beloveds I had endured much worse pains in the past, I slowly penetrated Erastos' trained ring and spread him wide. My paws gripped his antlers and pulled him up to face me, now making the deer bounce off my length—no doubt giving Alcaeus behind us a sight to behold. However, this did not distract him for long, not when a god consented to submit himself to a mortal.

He slipped a few times from excitement, yet the third try allowed our lion to probe me, impatiently entering me and causing my back to arch from his massive cock.

"Who is the kitten now, Apollo?" he nipped my ear, eliciting another moan from me.

I simply smirked back to him. "Prove it, little kitten."

His paws gripped my hips and he did not hold back, letting his dominant nature ravage me. I gasped at the dual sensation of a mortal lion's shaft pumping in and out of me while I vigorously did the same to a lithe deer accepting my own manhood. All at once, I made Erastos mine and allowed myself to be Alcaeus'.

We were a god bound between two mortals. Three now become one.

Unfortunately, the act itself did not last long. We were too lost in our lovemaking. Alcaeus' purrs twisted into snarls as he dug his claws into my hips, his thrusting pushing my cock deeper inside an equally dazed Erastos. His lips bruised mine and before either of us could prevent it, my red knot slipped into his stretched rear, and I drained my divine seed right as the mortal lion mounting me impatiently thrust one final time.

We were fatigued and collapsed together onto the sheets. Our panting and musk filled the bedroom. Our humid bodies lay together covered in sweat and stained seed, gulping in breaths from what had to be the best sexual experience any of us ever had.

Yes, including me.

Minutes later, I ignored my sore muscles (especially from under my matted tail) and pulled the three of us into a mutual embrace. We wordlessly cuddled together as I slowly licked each of their noses, staring into their loving eyes without blinking even once.

"You are the loves I have searched for all these centuries," I whispered to them. "I love you both, Alcaeus and Erastos of Dion…."

"I love you too, Apollo," Erastos whispered to our lion, "and I love you, Alcaeus."

He simply, huskily whispered back, "Me too."

The three of us giggled and relaxed into our arms and the soft bedsheets.

The planned wedding banquet days later would be attended by many, mortals and immortals alike. Besides the other Olympians, Alcaeus' well-adorned parents and siblings appeared alongside Erastos' father—who, shocked at first by my mere existence, dropped to his knees before his son in deep apology. Now the elder stag watched in tears of joy as his son was given a goblet of nectar and a clump of ambrosia.

Erastos and Alcaeus…they were so handsome that day. Athena gifted the latter a robe woven from the golden fleece of sun sheep, a small chlamys stitched alongside it as a wedding present from Hades. When I asked why he would bother making such a gift, my mysterious uncle simply said, "My Queen insisted. Besides, I am proud my nephew has found true love like I have…"

As for our Erastos, he proudly wore an elegant, silvery robe fastened together by a golden pin in the shape of a bow and arrow, as a gift from Artemis, who had earlier endlessly boasted about chaining myself down to not one but two lovers. I did not care though, not when I saw the youthful stag place the ambrosia on his tongue, chew it and drink from the goblet without a second thought.

Alcaeus could not have acted impatient enough, and our deer knew it, so he gave the other clump of ambrosia and the goblet of nectar to him almost immediately. The black-maned lion plopped the ambrosia into his maw, not even to chew it, and drank the rest of the nectar down in one gulp.

"Congratulations!" Dionysus nearby certainly voiced his approval.

The gathered and I laughed shortly, but I was already distracted by the sight of my beloveds, now marveling at their bodies starting to glow. My arms already wrapped around the duo when the crowd cheered.

Unbeknownst to anyone, the cheeky Erastos slipped his paws beneath our robes to stroke his newlywed husbands' cocks. His godly touch certainly had us stiffen immediately. I managed to silence my moans while Alcaeus barely resisted the temptation. Luckily, I found the brilliant idea to pull the lion to my lips, then the deer to mine.

Crying together we all finally shared a romantic kiss as equals.

Zeus laughed heartedly, raising his cup high. "Let us give our blessings to this glorious day, and welcome to Mount Olympus: Erastos, the God of Archery and Knowledge! And Alcaeus, the God of Poetry and Athletes!"

The Anniversary Gift

Linnea "LiteralGrill" Capps

———

[Tall Gal Cal] Oh yeah you had a date today! How was it?

[Daniel.exe] Eh… It wasn't bad I guess but I don't really want to see him again.

[Tall Gal Cal] Oh heck, what happened? Was he being a jerk? Because I'll totally fly over there and punch a jerk for you!

[Daniel.exe] Okay I'm going to just be honest here. The whole time I was out on that date? I kept thinking about how much better it would be if I was out on a date with you.

———

It had been two years to the date since Daniel had mustered up the courage to tell Calanthe how he really felt. He was reading over old messages while he waited for the little green dot by her name to turn green signalling she'd gotten online. Calanthe had promised the bunny an 'ultra special anniversary gift extravaganza,' and he was curious what she had planned. Even all this time later, going over those messages made warmth swell through his chest until his cheeks felt flushed under his white fur.

Daniel had known he felt connected to her ever since they had met in a boardgaming CableGram group chat. The only reason Daniel hadn't asked to date her earlier was the distance between them. With her living in the United States and him in Hungary he had thought it would be unfair to put pressure on her to date with over 7,000 kilometers between them. If things went well, someday one of them would have to leave the life they knew behind to immigrate to a new country. He hadn't wanted her to feel pressured to make such an enormous decision.

So when she had admitted that was the exact reason she hadn't asked him out yet either? The two had laughed before deciding distance or not it was worth seeing where their feelings led. So she had talked to her current boyfriend at the time to make sure he knew and was comfortable going forward, and their relationship had blossomed after.

He had known Calanthe was polyamorous when he had asked of course. Some of his friends had teased him about his girlfriend having another boyfriend and him being a 'side piece', but it hadn't bothered him. Especially with how far they were away it almost seemed more practical. She could have someone closer by for when she needed hugs, cuddles, or any other physical intimacy he couldn't provide. At the same time he could find someone to do the same though he hadn't felt the need to yet.

A green dot, she was online! Time zones could always be tricky, but she was running particularly late. Had it taken that long for her to set up the surprise? She had insisted that he didn't have to send her anything in return with how expensive shipping costs could be across the sea. He had used an online service to get a book she'd been wanting delivered from inside the US but if Calanthe had really gone all out maybe he should have done more.

A perky call song chirped and popped into his floppy ears. There wasn't any time left to think about that now; she was trying to start the call! He checked to make sure his webcam was plugged in and clicked to accept.

"Happy anniversary my little cutie!"

The joy rang through her voice and shown fiercely across her features. It was too infectious to ignore, Daniel flashing a buck-toothed grin.

"Happy anniversary yourself gorgeous!"

She hadn't been lying when she called him a *little* cutie, at least in comparison to herself. Her camera was set to face her bed so she could comfortably get her face into the picture while lying on her belly with just how long her neck was. Before he had seen her on camera she had always joked about how tall she was with Daniel telling her the truth that he had always found taller animals attractive.

When he had learned she was a giraffe, literally as tall as a girl could get, he had practically fallen out of his chair. He didn't know exactly how he had won the cosmic lottery in such a way, but he was not about to complain. He took a moment to admire the patchwork quilt of chestnut brown patches that patterned her cream-colored fur. Calanthe had told him each giraffe's spots were unique like a snowflake. He couldn't imagine a more perfect pattern than her own.

"Daniel? You're getting that dreamy look you get; stooooop!"

He could hear just how flattered she was despite her teasing tone. The hare had long since given up being embarrassed by just how often he found himself getting caught up in her beauty. Those long lashes, her sky blue eyes, even when she stuck out her purple tongue to poke fun at him like she was now he found her precious.

"Listen, looking at you is obviously the greatest anniversary gift in existence so let me enjoy it!"

Calanthe bashfully used a hoof to flick a tuft of her bangs to the side raising an eyebrow.

"Come on, if you keep feeding me compliments I'll just be a giggling happy mess! The ultra special anniversary gift extravaganza has to go on as planned!"

The two of them laughed together until the sound of a door opening and a third voice calling out interrupted them.

"Hey Cal, sounds like you got the new camera set up nice?"

A new camera? Daniel could notice it was a much higher quality feed than usual. More importantly, was that Garret talking?

Calanthe had originally been dating another giraffe, Landon, when the two of them had gotten together. Landon had never really opened up and talked to Daniel no matter how much he tried, not to mention he seemed to stay just as reserved with Calanthe not always being honest with how he felt.

Daniel had thought Garret, her newer boyfriend, was a vast improvement. He always went out of his way to listen to her problems and offer help whenever she needed it. The black bear even took time to chat with Daniel every day too, and they had a lot in common! The rabbit had considered asking Garret if he might like to make their V of a polycule into a triad proper a few times but hadn't yet gained the courage.

"Oh yeah I got it set up honey bear! You can see almost my whole room now!"

Daniel's nose twitched rapidly as he tried to figure out this odd puzzle presented to him. Why would she invite her other boyfriend over on the special day between them? He couldn't have anything to do with the surprise planned, unless… Was she really planning to do that today?

One of his long feet began to thump in nervous anticipation. When they had first gotten together, Calanthe had asked about how best to make him comfortable when it came to discussing sex with other partners. Long distance or not she insisted that he had enough information to have well informed consent in their own encounters.

At first they had taken things very slow, simply saying something happened the previous night, a discussion about comfort with being fluid bonded, but then there was the day he noticed the small mark on her long and slender neck.

She could have easily played it off as just fur brushed slightly wrong, but he felt positive it was made by a fang, maybe a claw. She had definitely been with someone, but the jealousy he had expected never came. Was it just curiosity? No, this was crackling just under the surface of his fur, an excited static rippling through his body, impossible to ignore.

So for the first time he asked for details, and for the first time he felt the heat seeping into his body as she told him. Every mention of a kiss, his heart raced, every touch and position recalled made his heart race. By the end the static beneath his fur had erupted so powerfully his blood was buzzing.

It took every ounce of focus to keep his paw off his throbbing length until their video call had ended. He had barely lasted a minute before warmth was splattering across his own chest.

At first he was embarrassed, but he had never been so excited before, he wanted her to share more stories. When his hunger could no longer be ignored he confessed to her what had happened. Instead of being teased or admonished she ended up being encouraging. So much so she told another story and demanded that he enjoy himself thoroughly on camera while she watched.

Once ignited, these passions wouldn't simmer out, and Calanthe was curious what was fueling it. Something deep inside him found some masochistic pleasure knowing she was having sex with another man. A man that was close by and could actually touch and hold her unlike him. They had figured out he had a kink for cuckolding.

Now Garret was in the room with his girlfriend on their night of their anniversary, and Daniel could see he was caressing her rump with his big bear paw.

They had talked about trying to make a scene for real. Garret was much larger and stronger than Daniel could ever hope to be and a predator to boot. In any other situation he may have been too jealous to enjoy this 'superior man' he knew would be fucking his girlfriend right in front of him on his anniversary no less.

Here he knew all it would take is to say yellow and things would slow down, red and they would stop completely. Here he had a loving girlfriend he knew he could trust and a metamour he cared deeply for. Whatever words were said, whatever actions taken, were just part of the scene. A scene that had his whiskers twitching in anticipation for it to begin.

"Hey you're looking a bit twitchy there Dan, you doing okay?"

The bear gave him a knowing smirk, punctuating his question with a firm grope of Calanthe's ass.

"I just u-um, thought it would j-just be Calanthe and m-me today."

The bear let out a deep chuckle at Daniel's fumbling of his words. "Well you see, I thought Cal here deserved a proper gift for your anniversary today. Something I'm far better equipped to do."

His paw was slowly creeping up underneath Calanthe's shirt, her shivering at the teasing touch. The bear was slowly going for her bra, taking his time to be sure there was no way Daniel could miss him unclipping it. Garret's cocky grin was just begging for a comment, for a plea for him to stop that would most certainly be ignored. Still the hare couldn't resist taking the bait.

"H-Hey what are you doing? Did you forget you're on camera?"

"Oh I know I'm on camera, I know I'm going to fuck Cal senseless, and I know you're too much of a wimp to actually stop me even if you were here in person. Not that you'd want to, I can see your paw moving towards your cock right now!"

Daniel whimpered in surprise; he hadn't expected the bear would notice his paw had slipped off his desk and was creeping under.

"You put that paw back on the desk. If either of your paws leave the desk again, I end the call, and you're stuck imagining just how hard I'll be plowing your girlfriend. Got it?"

He gulped and nodded, too excited to even speak. The bear wasted no time, using his claws to her shirt down the back. Calanthe shot Garret a playful but pouty look over her shoulder at her shirt being destroyed before he flipped her onto her back. The now ruined shirt slid to reveal her chest, her breasts only briefly exposed before the bear grasped them in his paws.

"So soft, and all mine…"

Garret leaned down, and his muzzle met the giraffe's,

tongues rolling over each other as carnal moans escaped their lips. The bear climbed on top of her, his paws moving from her breasts to pin her arms down onto the bed over her head. As they looked into each others' eyes with blazing passion Daniel was stuck with his paws on the desk, cock throbbing, unable to do anything but watch.

Their hips were grinding together, Garret moving from kissing Calanthe to nipping on her long slender neck with a growl. She squeaked and squirmed as he bit down just hard enough to leave marks, little reminders for Daniel in the coming weeks of what was happening before him.

The hare refused to risk moving his paws once more but was desperate for some form of relief. There was serious friction from his hard cock causing a tent in his pants. Desperate for any attention to his throbbing member he tried to grind against his thighs. Pleasure splintered through his body, teasing him to new heights but getting him no closer to release.

As he struggled without the use of his paws the couple on his screen had no such issues. Their paws were free to grasp at each others' pants and underwear freeing themselves from the very prison he found himself trapped in. When Garret's length sprung free Daniel's jaw dropped. He knew his own dick was a bit above average for a rabbit, but it was nothing compared to massive bear cock.

Daniel couldn't take his eyes off it. He was certain it was so thick one of his paws alone couldn't wrap around it. Twitching, throbbing, that same cock was now sliding against Calanthe's warm folds as she squirmed and pleaded for him to thrust it inside.

"Come on stop teasing, I finally have a chance to get fucked by a decent sized cock so put it in me!"

That humiliating jab left the hare breathless. He wanted to be exploring her warm depths, making her cry out in ecstasy with every thrust. Instead the slick sounds each movement of their hips caused left him dizzy, drunk from just how badly he wished he could warm his own shaft in his paw. Her back was arching, legs wrapping around Garret's back, doing everything she could to get the bear's cock further inside. They had played with themselves in front of the camera before, but Daniel had never been able to get her moaning as loud as Garret could before. He was being utterly outclassed and loving every minute of it.

"Come on, breed me! I need your cum inside me!"

The bear's claws sank into the bed, his breath hitching at the encouragement. Daniel's hips bucked in his seat, an overwhelming desire to reach climax alongside the couple mounting. The two were entirely oblivious to his pathetic whimpering, entranced in their own world of pleasure.

The bear let out an unmistakable groan, and Daniel knew thick ropes of cum were being shot inside his girlfriend whose entire body was a shuddering mess of bliss. The hare could see the copious amounts of Garret's cum flooding out around his cock and couldn't hold back another second. Even the feeble rubbing of his thighs was finally effective, pleasure rocketing through his body as he creamed his pants.

The three of them gasped for breath, hearts racing in their chests. The bear gently laid himself down on top of the giraffe, chuckling softly.

"Okay Dan, you can use your paw now."

"I w-well um, d-don't need to anymore…"

Caranthe grinned, looking a bit light-headed. "Oh my gosh it was that good? I knew I was having fun, but dang that was a good performance Garret."

The three began to laugh, the scene obviously coming to an end. Garret went to grab a towel to clean up, Calanthe taking a moment to make absolutely sure everything was okay.

"We didn't cross any boundaries right? I know this was a bit of a surprise, but I want to make sure everything was still good for you. It is your anniversary gift after all. You know I love you so much and your body, especially that part of it, is incredibly sexy right?"

The hare couldn't help but smile. Even now she wanted him to know all the teasing about a decent-sized cock was only that: teasing.

"I love you too Calanthe, and obviously you're gorgeous!

Well honestly you both are."

Garret had returned just in time to hear, his ears upturned in pride from the compliment.

"You know speaking of my being gorgeous…I did have a thought before we started all this."

"Oh? What was that?" The hare tilted his head, curious.

"Well especially if you find me gorgeous, I'd been thinking…I do really like you Dan, and I'd love to do something like this more often. You know, something with the three of us and not just sexy things!"

Daniel's whiskers twitched once more, unsure of where he was going. Sensing this was the case, Garret continued.

"I mean…Just thought it'd be easier to remember your anniversaries maybe if they were both on the same date. Y-You know if you wanted…"

Garret stuttering? The bunny could hardly believe what he heard. Not only had he experienced one of the best sexual moments of his life, the guy he had been getting up the courage to ask out had beaten him to the punch!

"Yes, absolutely yes!"

Calanthe clapped her hooves together in excitement. "Oh my gosh this is so weirdly romantic; I love it! We gotta get you here for a visit Daniel!"

"I agree," Garret replied. "It would be way more fun to do this in person after all. Plus I want to squish you with a hug so bad right now!"

The three continued talking, everyone in high spirits, until it was finally too late for Daniel to stay up any longer in his time zone. The call had to end, Daniel had to clean himself up and get some sleep. As he drifted off to slumber he smiled, knowing his two favorite people in the world were basking in the afterglow of their sexcapade and cuddling together and that in a few months he might be able to hop on a plane and join them.

Bios

ANHEDRAL is proudly Canadian by birth, but was raised in England, where he studied zoology. After moving to Scotland he made a career in ecology and conservation, but these days he's a music teacher and an aspiring writer, and he's loving it.

Anhedral remained shamefully ignorant of the creative maelstrom that is furry until 2012. A kindly wolf and a lovely fennec helped him to catch up, and their warmth and generosity showed the fandom at its truest and its best. The writer's wife suffers his newfound addiction with bemused tolerance, and for her love and support he remains extremely grateful.

When he's not wrestling unruly sentences or scaring his flute students with unplayable duets, Anhedral enjoys cycling, hill-walking, and carting his camera to out-of-the-way places. He drinks too much coffee for his own good, will never have time to get through all of the brilliant fantasy and science fiction on his bucket list, and has a weakness for most any critter that can fly. Most of his scribbles can be found over at http://www.furaffinity.net/user/anhedral/. His short stories have also appeared in 'ROAR' volume 10 and in 'Werewolves Versus The Circus'.

CEDRIC G! BACON has been a writer most of his life, and since 2017 has been submitting stories to various publications. He works the front desk at a Holiday Inn hotel chain, and in his spare time he enjoys reading comic books, photography (specifically those of action figures), collecting action figures, watching Doctor Who (both Classic and New), and of course creating new stories. He has appeared in *Infurno*, *Slashers*, *Thrill of the Hunt*, *12 Days of Yiffmas*, *Furry Trash*, and *Sinister Sheets*.

He currently lives in North Florida with his girlfriend and two cats.

LINNEA "LITERALGRILL" CAPPS is a three-time August Derleth award winning poet and Leo Literary Award winning author. She has also been nominated for the Ursa Major Awards.

She's also a smoking hot grill on the internet constantly getting up to shenanigans and out exploring the world. When not seeking out adventures and experiences, she happily plays songs on her ukulele and writes the stories she dreams up every night before bed. You can find her on Twitter @LiteralGrill or on her website www.linneacapps.com

NATHAN HOPP was born and raised in Green Bay, WI. He's been writing furry fiction since high school, and since meeting his first boyfriend through the fandom in college, has experienced the joys and hardships of love. When he isn't trying too hard to write the next great American novel, Nathan loves to read, play Minecraft, go on bike rides and read about Ancient Greek mythology in his spare time.

Hi! I'm **PATRICK D. LAMBERT**. Writer. Crocodile. And fervent believer that love shall be shared with everyone. But even for someone who is currently on a polyamorous relationship, finding the right words to express what I think and feel about it it's a complex task, as words alone can't describe a feeling that it's different for everyone—which doesn't mean I won't try. So I put aside the demons, madness and irrepressible lust that are a big part of my usual work to share with all of you the vision I have of love: sweet, kinky, and definitely spontaneous. Feel free to contact me on Twitter as @ProfeLambert, especially if my interpretation of a poly relation catches your attention.

www.ingramcontent.com/pod-product-compliance
Lightning Source LLC
Chambersburg PA
CBHW070913160726
48004CB00003B/1356